Easy Streets

EASY STREETS

Bill James

W. W. NORTON & COMPANY

New York • London

For information about permission to reproduce selections from this book, write
to Permissions, W. W. Norton & Company, Inc., 500 Fifth Avenue, New York,
NY 10110

Manufacturing by RR Donnelley, Haddon Division
Production manager: Julia Druskin

Library of Congress Cataloging-in-Publication Data

James, Bill, date.
    Easy streets / Bill James.—1st American ed.
    p. cm.
    ISBN 0-393-06042-X
    1. Harpur, Colin (fictitious character)—Fiction. 2. Iles, Desmond (Fictitious
character)—Fiction. 3. Police—Great Britain—Fiction. 4. Police corruption—
Fiction. 5. Drug traffic—Fiction. I. Title.

PR6070.U23E17 2005
823'914—dc22   2005047306

W. W. Norton & Company, Inc.
500 Fifth Avenue, New York, N.Y. 10110
www.wwnorton.com

W. W. Norton & Company Ltd.
Castle House, 75/76 Wells Street, London W1T 3QT

1 2 3 4 5 6 7 8 9 0

Chapter One

Watching as the girl's body was brought out, or what was left of it, Iles said: 'Know that poem, Col – "A refusal to mourn the death by fire of a child"?'

'Poetry's always been one of your things, sir,' Harpur replied.

'*I* don't refuse to mourn.'

'Well, you wouldn't.'

'Dylan Thomas. Talks about the "majesty" of her death.'

'Many a poet gets away with shit, sir,' Harpur said. 'They like words with y on the end. Give a nice tinkle. That's what interests them. But you – you can be surprisingly tender and sympathetic. I've heard one or two people mention that. Two.'

'OK, Col, some low-life's kid is burned, a nobody pusher's kid. But still a cherished child.'

Yes, Iles could be surprisingly tender and sympathetic. Perhaps he was thinking of a similar scene when the body of a lover of his was recovered from a burned building looking, as he'd put it, like 'a slab of charred turf'.* Now, they stood with a little group of spectators in the dark behind a blue and white barrier tape slung between two street lamp pillars. The house fire was as good as beaten. One hose still played, but only a damping down job. Most of the crowd had gone home to bed.

'If it's arson I suppose you'd –'

'Of course it's fucking arson,' the Assistant Chief replied.

* *Halo Parade*

5

'If it's arson I suppose you'd claim this fits your chaos theme, sir?' Harpur said.

'No, I wouldn't claim that, Harpur. I don't crow – any more than I refuse to mourn.'

'Sorry, sir, but I've often heard you crow. You do like a triumph – need to be right. Like all of us. Crowing's one of your passions.'

They'd got some sort of grey sheeting around the child, bulky, stiff and approximate, nothing like a properly con-toured body-bag, and now a plain green van backed up slowly between the fire tenders, its rear doors already open and swinging gently. Two firemen put the bundle inside on the floor and closed the doors. The ambulance moved away. 'Now and then it's true I might crow, Col,' the ACC said. 'I choose the occasion when I crow. This is not one of the occasions when I'd crow. For instance, Harpur, I might have crowed when my wife decided that the rotten carry-on with you – backs of cars, broom cupboards, flop-house hotels – yes, when Sarah decided it was over and a full return to me followed.' Iles had begun to more or less scream now and frothed a bit, as he generally did when referring to his wife and Harpur. One of the firemen who had dealt with the body, his face streaked by ash, was about to re-enter the house and glanced over at Iles, but would think the din grief. Iles had on a brown bomber jacket and crimson scarf worn loosely and nobody who didn't know would identify him as an Assistant Chief Constable. 'Look here, Harpur, I want to assure you, really assure you, that these days, when Sarah refers to you and that episode, she's amazed she could ever have imagined –'

'When I spoke of chaos, I meant what you were talking about earlier, at my house, sir.'

'Col, I know what you meant. And do you believe I want my thoughts turned into something like this?' Iles said. He gave a brief, shivering wave towards the small, scorched house.

His thoughts. Plenty of those. Before the Control Room phone call that brought him and Harpur here tonight, the

6

ACC had run through a few of them, seated sideways in one of Harpur's armchairs, legs over the armrest, feet duckily close. Iles was keen on his legs and black lace-ups. He'd said: 'We're watching the start of chaos, Col.'

'You sound like Mr Lane, the old Chief, sir,' Harpur replied. 'He always feared worldwide break-up, starting on our patch.'

'An uneasy mind.'

'You destroyed it and him, sir,' Harpur said.

'Oh, but it would give me true pain if I thought that, Col.'

'*Do* you think it, Mr Iles?' Harpur's younger daughter, Jill, asked. She had a really understanding side, as could happen with children for a while.

'I often recall him,' Iles replied. 'Mark Lane was the sort who could listen tolerantly, patiently to all sorts and then after a remarkably short while form his own clear, uncluttered overview. Naturally, this would always be catastrophically wrong, but authentic, absolutely the Chief's or his wife's.'

They had been talking in the big sitting room of Harpur's house at 126 Arthur Street. Although Iles generally spoke of the address as a slum, disgustingly unfit to raise children in, he would often visit for confidential, unofficial talks about police things and to show off his garments, shoes and profile to Harpur's older daughter, Hazel. Both girls liked Iles and, obviously, Harpur could not keep him away from them absolutely and permanently. Hazel and Jill still believed that hidden a fair way down Iles had something very close to wholesomeness, despite how he seemed. Occasionally, Harpur thought they might be right, or almost half right, but he had to worry that this wholesomeness lay buried so well it might not have a chance against Iles's more standard lout side – like the tenderness and sympathy.

'Chaos how?' Harpur had asked.

'Permissiveness,' Iles replied.

'Which?' Harpur said.

'Which? *Which?*' Iles said.

7

'Drugs?' Harpur said.

'Softening the law on use and dealing, for the sake of street peace, plus recognition that substance trading can't be stopped, anyway,' Iles replied. 'Surrender. Bumper tolerance. Chief Constables preach it these days. Even that sweet-voiced jerk, the Home Secretary, preaches it. But do they long-view things, Col?'

'In which respect, sir?'

'More of the stuff about, so a buyers' market. Easy access brings the price down. People like Ralphy Ember, Manse Shale, Sashaying Vernon, Ferdy Dubal – if he wasn't recently so dead – others, all running, or having run, gorgeous, profitable supply firms of varying size, suddenly find their incomes hacked. Response? They decide – this answer is forced on them, Col – however much they might want to behave sweetly – forced on them by reason and need – they decide there's only enough business for one, maybe two, so the task is, eliminate the others. War. Carnage. Obviously, I don't object to carnage where the sods kill one another or get truly permanent, disabling wounds. The harmless and innocent can get caught by it, though.' Harpur thought of the words later on that night when Lorraine Sambrook was put into the van.

During the earlier discussion in his sitting room, Harpur had said: 'But when Mr Lane commanded here you let them run their firms, regardless of the Chief's objections, and even Mrs Lane's. Wouldn't you call that permissiveness, tolerance? Sir.'

The Assistant Chief laughed silently for a due spell. Besides the tenderness and sympathy, he could summon a kind of brilliant, warm delicacy and tact few expected from someone with his high rank, egomaniac eyes and domineering soul. He would never call Harpur a stupid cunt in front of his daughters, still only schoolchildren of twelve and fifteen. But he did laugh silently for a due time as though startled and amused at meeting a stunted brain unashamed to show just *how* stunted. 'Ralphy and Manse et cetera knew they had to act civilized, no mayhem, or I'd take away their privileged spots. An agreement – tacit but

8

strong. Thus, tranquil streets, even tranquil back lanes and high-rise staircases. There won't *be* any privileged spots once the price drops. They'll try to kill each other as a step to monopoly. Free market imperatives – the most imperative imperatives known to man, Col.'

Harpur was a single parent and recognized a big duty to his daughters, especially Hazel, now fifteen and emerging a bit, the way they did around that age. The brown leather bomber jacket and crimson scarf with tassels was an ensemble Iles often put on for these calls, and Harpur wondered if Hazel had told him she liked it. He looked like a star amateur dramatics actor, or the owner of a middle grade bric-a-brac shop inclined to go on about his 'delight in small, beautiful things'. You couldn't expect Hazel to have developed proper taste yet. Iles did not remove the scarf indoors.

Jill said: 'As a matter of fact, some kids at school reckon you let Ember and Shale, and maybe the others, but definitely Ralph Ember and Shale – you let them run their firms because they gave you a good dab in the hand, Mr Iles.'

'This is the way kids are,' Iles replied.

'Which kids at school? I've never heard kids at school talk like that about him,' Hazel said.

'Oh, my, has someone spoken roughly about dear Desmond?' Jill replied, in a big, mock-caring voice.

'Which kids at school?' Hazel asked.

'They're not going to say it to *you*, are they?' Jill replied.

'Why aren't they going to say it to me, dandruff queen?' Hazel asked.

'You know why they're not going to say it to you,' Jill replied.

'No, why aren't they going to say it to me?'

'Because they know Desmond Iles is –'

'Probably it would be best if you two went into the other room and did some TV now,' Harpur said.

'Know Desmond Iles is what?' Hazel said.

'If you were on the take, Mr Iles, you'd hate the law to ease up on drugs because Ember and Shale wouldn't need protection any more,' Jill replied. 'End of bribes. This is what they say.'

'These are thoughtful children,' Iles replied.

'*I* don't believe you've been on the take,' Jill said. 'I always defend you.'

'Where?' Iles asked.

'School – the yard.'

'Oh, the Merciful and All-Seeing One hath spoken,' Hazel fluted.

'Thanks, Jill,' Iles replied.

She said: 'But what they keep on about – I thought you ought to know it as an Assistant Chief and so on because it's maybe what they hear from their parents –'

'And possibly from the staff?' Iles asked.

'*Quid pro quoism*, in Latin,' Jill replied. 'You scratch my back, I'll stay off yours. They say you've got the big house in Rougemont Place, a beautiful wife who dresses catwalk, a baby you'll want a private school for later – therefore you need back-handers,' Jill replied. 'And the big dealers can afford to pay – so far. The tale is, Shale and Ember skim more than half a big one each.'

'I wish you wouldn't talk movie scripts,' Harpur said.

'The tale is, Ember and Shale pay themselves more than half a million a year each,' Jill replied. The telephone in the hall had rung then and she stood up and went to take the call.

'You know what kids of her age are like,' Hazel said. 'All they do is pick holes. They have no idea what policing is about – how it works.'

'You're patient with her, Hazel,' Iles said. 'I admire that in you. One of many fine qualities which add up to a uniqueness. Oh, yes.'

'"Dab in the hand". I mean, so crude,' Hazel said.

'I've had worse said about me,' Iles replied.

'Certainly,' Harpur remarked.

'What?' Hazel asked.

'It comes with the office,' Iles said.

'What? *What* do they say?' Hazel asked.

Jill returned. It was the Control Room wanting Harpur.

They wouldn't tell her why, although she'd tried to get it out of them. When he took the call they said a fire at Curly Sambrook's place on the Ernest Bevin council estate and possibly dubious. Curly and his girlfriend had burns and were in hospital. Their daughter, Lorraine, aged five, might still be inside. Curly had tried to save her. Harpur prepared to leave. 'You'd better come, sir,' he told Iles, though without saying where and why while the children listened.

The ACC said: 'Oh, I think I'll stay and –'

'You'd better come, sir,' Harpur replied.

'Something important?' Jill asked. 'Has to be. They wouldn't call out a mighty and majestic Detective Chief Super at this time of night otherwise.'

'Go to bed at eleven o'clock if I'm not back,' Harpur said. 'Denise can't sleep here tonight.'

'Ah, that still going on, Col, you and the lovely undergraduate?' Iles said.

'She *is* lovely, isn't she, Mr Iles?' Jill replied. 'And yet she doesn't seem to worry about how dad looks, or his age or haircut or music or clothes, she still wants him. It's sweet. She's really cleaned up his life, you know. I used to worry about him. I expect you did.'

'We like it when Denise is here for breakfast,' Hazel said.

'That would be most days?' Iles asked.

'Just like a family,' Jill replied.

'Tonight she has to stay in the student residence because there's a leaving party for one of the staff,' Harpur said.

'I believe her,' Jill said. 'She's young and all those other students around, but I think she sticks by dad. I do.' She nodded hard a few times. 'Important how, though – this call-out, dad? Dangerous? Weapons? You tooled up? Of course you're not, either of you. British police just play at it.'

'Go to bed at eleven o'clock and don't open the door,' Harpur said.

'I might look in to check you're all right, if your father has to stay at the scene,' Iles said. 'Whatever it is.'

'Don't open the door,' Harpur said.

At Curly's house now, a carpenter arrived to board up the house and secure it. The front door had been smashed by firemen on their way in when first called, and most of the windows were gone. Iles said: 'The point is, Col, poets think they have a duty to find the positive side about rough factors like death – *especially* death. This is one of their topics. Remember those lines from "For the Fallen".'

'You've got a bucketful of them, sir.'

'About young soldiers killed in the First War –

'They shall not grow old, as we that are left grow old:
Age shall not weary them.'

'But they *wanted* to grow old, or older, anyway,' Harpur replied. 'Lorraine Sambrook wanted to grow older.'

'With your sort of mind you'd be stuck for subjects if you were a poet, Harpur.'

'We ought to go and try to talk to Curly or his partner,' Harpur replied. They drove to Paston Hospital, but Curly had died and the girlfriend was not interviewable at present and, probably, not for at least weeks doctors told them, supposing she lived.

Harpur took Iles back to his own car, parked in Arthur Street. The house was dark, thank God. 'Or then there's Donne, of course,' the ACC said:

'Death, be not proud, though some have called thee
Mighty and dreadful, for thou art not so.'

'Death doesn't do too badly, though,' Harpur said.

'Did Curly grass?'

'Not to me.'

'In general.'

'I'd need to speak to the drugs squad.'

'But he was dealing, was he – small-time, freelance? Who was his wholesaler?' Iles replied.

'I'd need to speak to the drugs squad.'

'Do you ever answer anything? We've nabbed Sashaying Vernon for something, haven't we, Col?'

'Awaiting trial. In the new climate, he'll probably get bail.'

'Where did our information come from?'

'That's always a tricky one, sir.'

'And, then, above all Emily Dickinson as poet – American,' Iles replied. 'Death as a kind of considerate chum:

'Because I could not stop for Death –
He kindly stopped for me.'

Harpur said: 'And now he's kindly stopped for Curly and the child.'

Chapter Two

The thing about Ralph Ember was he definitely did not mind nuns, could definitely say he had no prejudice, but some situations they would never be able to cope with and he flew out from Stansted to Bordeaux. Obviously, with the X-rays and frisking you could carry nothing serious on a plane these days, especially after September 11 2001, but that was all right as he reckoned there would be no call for armament at any stage. Ember felt nearly sure nobody outside his family even knew he was going. It should be a totally peaceful, educational trip. For God's sake, of course it should. He wanted a look around, an update look around, that was all.

He flew standard. He hated this, because of the kind of people and their clothes and so on. If you went pricey, though, it could draw attention – you élited yourself. He would do standard again on the return, whether or not he brought Venetia with him. That would depend on what he thought as a result of the look around out there in France. His guess was she *would* be with him. Too bad if she kicked up at standard. This whole move was about her safety and nothing else, so she'd better fucking understand. A teenager. If Ralph said standard she'd take standard, and no hoity-toity.

Naturally, he'd cased the school she was at in France when they first entered her there, but matters had deteriorated again in the trade scene at home since, with very rough deaths, and now he needed to do some really close checks in case one of his enemies or in case one of his supposed chums thought of Venetia out in France. Christ,

14

though, that terrible stuff with Curly Sambrook and his family – and Curly such a nothing in the trade.

It was not just the security of the school buildings and grounds and over-accessibility at Venetia's school that troubled Ralph. He wanted to know what the pupils did in their time off, where they went, whether they were supervised and had some protection. Exactly what he meant about nuns. Although a lot of them might be all right and totally unabusive, they were not roughhouse-trained. Ember blamed nobody for that. You had to be reasonable. Full-out, battle-hard minding was no nun role. If one of those invading outfits who wanted to push Ralph's firm under sent out a heavy or two from Britain for Venetia the school staff might try to guard her, but would have no real chance. Or if one of the outfits apparently *co-operating* with Ralph's sent out a heavy or two. Nuns had been taught to believe in prayer and candles. Prayer was certainly fine and had a good background in the Bible, but could fail against hired villains, or fail to work fast enough in matters of this life, not the next.

Lately, worried by the sudden terrible spell of trade problems, brutalities and executions at home, Ember had begun to think Venetia might be exposed at that Bordeaux school. Someone could decide to squeeze Ralph by pouching one of his adored daughters and jailing her in a secret Euro cellar, with video appeals to pressure and smash him. Many cellars undoubtedly existed in France on account of the wine and gourmet mushrooms. He spotted the hazard early and as soon as the downturn and the violence started he'd transferred her very quietly – or he *thought* very quietly – from a finishing school in Poitiers to this one. But people would show in conversation they knew where she was, even after the change, and not people he had told or ever would. Well, would he? *And Venetia, Ralph – still at the French polishing establishment on the noble Garonne?* Why would they pay trackers to find her like that if they didn't plan something?

Ralph was familiar with Bordeaux and really liked it. A lot of Britishness. We had owned it once, and there was still a British bookshop. Many British wine drinkers revered Bordeaux for its claret, and he had come previously himself on trips to buy vintages for his club, the Monty, in its future role. Some vineyards were even Brit owned and top rate, such as Château de Sours. It did not outrage Ralph at all that Bordeaux tarts were already sitting outside on respectable-looking kitchen chairs in several streets when he arrived today at noon. A port had tides and sailors needing to fit in opportunities.

Originally, the distance from Britain had seemed to help with Venetia's safety, but he'd come to feel it didn't really. She was more vulnerable out here than even Curly and his household. An instructed lad or lads could nip across the water and see to her. All right, like Ember, he, or they, would not be able to carry anything, but those behind him, them, might arrange for him, them, to be met and armed on a loan basis, and then he'd, they'd, dispose or hand it or them over before the return journey. Probably a gun, guns, would only be used to keep the nuns quiet and prayerful, while Venetia was taken – no actual firing, just a frightener, but enough.

Ember had decided to visit and if he found weaknesses and likely danger in the Bordeaux set-up he would bring her back at once so he and his people could see to well-being in a charted setting. No bugger who knew Ralph Ember and Ralph Ember's power would be idiot enough to try arson on his fine home, Low Pastures. Probably he could get Venetia back into the local private place where his younger daughter, Fay, went as a day girl. It was quite a decent outfit although they did not do Latin and Greek, only classical tales in damn English, such as Atalanta's fucking apples with crummy illustrations. In one of his protests about dodging off the real tongues like that he had asked the head whether a Latin phrase existed for 'dumbing down'. Ember didn't know any classical language himself, but was sure they meant quality, especially the significant Greek alphabet. Although he hadn't really intended Venetia should leave France yet, you had to watch changed circumstances and changed risk. Leadership and parenthood both demanded that. Ralph could never neglect these responsibilities.

He still thought it had been a sound idea to get her away overseas for a time after those untidy episodes here with older men when she was even younger, and not men Ralph could in any way admire, nor his wife, Margaret. Slouches or piffling villains. He chose the French convent-style spots, and with nuns, at real cost, so Venetia's galloping puberty could be hobbled for a while, and taste and decorum imposed via a Continental culture. Despite round-the-clock whoring here, everyone knew the French were traditional at getting legs-crossed coolness and sense into questing young girls from good families. To make use of this famed skill, he'd been willing to gamble that Venetia would not encounter holy sisters who fancied girl flesh themselves.

The Mother Superior at Venetia's school spoke tip-top English luckily. Ember said: 'I wonder whether you've had any inquiries about my daughter.'

'What kind of inquiries, Mr Ember?' He thought she looked all right in her gear, about fifty, small-nosed, big-toothed, thin-necked, unpimpled, cheerful, no saucy urges.

'At first, this would be inquiries to do with locating her.'

'And afterwards?'

'Have there been inquiries of that sort?' Ember asked.

'Let me assure you, we are used to dealing with such intrusions. Oh, certainly. We know some parents wish for confidentiality, indeed *require* confidentiality. We are sympathetic to that, entirely. One doesn't ask about their . . . well, *milieu.*'

'Background.'

'*Milieu.*'

'And *have* there been intrusions of that sort?' Ember asked.

'I would prefer to call them *attempted* intrusions.'

'Have there been attempted intrusions of that sort?'

'We do not keep a record of every attempted intrusion of

17

that sort because we have a procedure for dealing with such attempted intrusions instantly and finally and to record them all would be a redundancy.'

'What procedure?' Ember said.

'Simply to say that the pupil list is a private document and details are not disclosed willy-nilly.'

'How about *un*-willy-nilly?'

'Mr Ember?'

'So you might not know whether there have in fact been inquiries about Venetia? If no note is made.'

'Some of our parents are in extremely sensitive positions and occupations, Mr Ember – Paris, Lagos, Zagreb. We have a responsibility to them. I expect you, too, are in such a sensitive position. But one does not ask.'

'One has certain business concerns,' Ember said.

'Well, this goes without saying.'

'And would you inform parents if inquiries about one of the pupils *was* made – that is, if hitting them with the willy-nilly failed to stop their interest?'

'Certainly, should the inquiries persist. We understand the world, you know, Mr Ember. We realize it is not totally a rose garden.'

'And then when the girls have some time off – say the weekend. Would they go into Bordeaux? I know some grand shops there. M&S. Might they be unaccompanied?'

'Their timetable for such excursions is strict, Mr Ember. The school has its own people-carrier. They must report back there on the dot, absolutely on the dot, they know this.'

'Or possibly if people were noticed outside the school, observing a pupil. Maybe in the grounds. It's not difficult to enter. Would that be reported to you?'

The small nose twitched and cheerfulness was ditched. 'Evidently, as I've said, I would never ask what kind of business you are concerned with in your own country, since it is none of my concern in the least, oh, no, but do you fear people – your business associates, for example – might come looking for Venetia here in this way, Mr Ember?'

18

'Anything of that sort?'

'This would not be very good from my school's point of view. From the point of view of reputation, you see. People lurking.'

'I think of it from my daughter's point of view.'

'Other parents might become anxious if they thought possible marauders of that kind were drawn here by Venetia.'

'Have you heard of anything like that – hired fucks stalking her, you dodgy, fee-grabbing French *vache*?' he replied.

Ember disliked people from the other sides of his life turning up at the Monty. Obviously, he could not actually ban them from the club, but he tried to let such associates know in all sorts of ways that if they wanted a meeting with him about a project or a necessary cleansing, cleansings, it ought to be done somewhere else. He had very exact, loving plans for the Monty in the middle to long term, and these needed non-stop, sensitive care. He saw himself as into two kinds of business, and the club stood very separate from the rest.

This lad Denzil Lake should certainly not be here now. Ember detested Lake's suit. It was double-breasted, navy-to-black with a thick chalk stripe, three buttons to the jacket, all done up, and the top one almost at Lake's throat, sausage skin style. Maybe it was not true to say Ember detested the suit as a suit. But he thought it wrong for someone in Lake's category, offensively wrong. This tailoring a genuine royal duke might wear, or the owner of many unisex hairdressing salons, but Lake was only a fucking chauffeur basically, Mansel Shale's. All right, a chauffeur with some bodyguard, strong-arm and disposal duties, like all chauffeurs in a hard commercial . . . well, *milieu*, but when you got down to it still only a chauffeur and out of order in swagger garb.

Of course, Ember recognized that for Denzil to come here uninvited and dressed up like this might signify he wanted a hike in role and status, and thought Ralph could help. Someone craved an alliance. Ralph could smell it. He was used to approaches like this. Ralph always believed in looking beyond a mere incident or worsted cloth to what was *really* meant. Without making it a matter of vanity, Ember knew he had insight. Now, he wondered if he could spot in Denzil's high-born style an attempt at some new career plan. All right. This could conceivably be useful for Ralph. Denzil's suit might actually signify a get-rid project – get rid of Shale, his boss. Ralph could definitely see pluses in that as a business scenario. He did not object to listening, even to someone like Denzil. You had to be awake to influences, ideas, regardless of where they came from.

'So, this visit – something important, Denzil?' Ember asked.

'Oh, daddy, don't be so . . . well, head-on,' Venetia said.

All right, Ember would admit the Denzil suit and quite quiet tie might have their positive aspects for some, but it enraged him that Venetia seemed impressed by them and by Denzil Lake. This late afternoon, she happened to be with Ralph around the club, and now, for heaven's sake, look at her grinning and standing close, exceptionally front on and body-languaging to Lake. It was less than a week since Ralph brought her back from Bordeaux, yet already he could sense absolutely no temperateness or religion on her breath as she chatted weather to Denzil like a come-on code. Occasionally, Ember wondered if they had been stupid to pick the name Venetia. It was unusual and mysterious and seemed to push her into a certain sort of ripe and experimental behaviour from very early. He doubted if the convents had really got to grips with it. She might have grown up more governable if christened, say, Mandy or Christine, though that big cop Harpur apparently had a dodgy daughter of Venetia's age and *she* was called Hazel. *Hazel.* They said Desmond Iles yearned for her. God, an Assistant Chief Constable schoolgirling! Parenthood – such a load of angles.

'Many's the great warm day you enjoyed in Bordeaux, Venetia, no doubt,' Lake remarked.

'Oh, indeed, yes,' she replied.

'What's this visit about, Denzil?' Ember asked. 'Crucial? Some message from Manse?'

'Such as sitting outside cafés in the street with a citron-nade,' Lake replied.

'These were pleasant, typical interludes on Saturdays,' Venetia said.

'And possible quite late into the summer, owing to the high temperatures lingering,' Lake said.

'All that – it just becomes a normal aspect of life,' Venetia replied.

'Not here,' Lake said.

'Hardly,' Venetia said. 'Is summer on a Tuesday or Wednesday this year?'

'Right,' Lake replied. He chuckled for a time, and did not seem worried about showing those completely unmillennium teeth.

Ember said: 'What's on, Denzil? I've got to do some tidying up before the evening crowd arrives.' Lake had what Ember thought of as a chauffeur's face, a servant's face but selfish, and a little gone to the side because of having to talk with Shale over one shoulder when Manse was in the back of the car. Perhaps if a lot of your conversations were like that, not eye-to-eye, it might be easy to go for betrayal. All kind of huge changes were under way inside the firms during this flux period. Denzil had always been cocky and an opportunist and might believe he had a chance of toppling Manse and replacing him. Chauffeur one day, chairman the next. Possible?

'Well, I hope you can settle at home, all the same, Venetia, after the joys of France,' Lake said.

'I think so,' Venetia replied.

'Lovely name,' Lake said. 'I don't believe I ever come across it before.'

'Denzil being quite unusual also,' Venetia replied.

'I hope you don't let people call you Ven.'

'I hope you don't let people call you Den!'

21

They had a joint laugh over this for a time. A scheme like Denzil's, if he had one, would definitely be advantageous for Ralph, played right, and as long as he, personally, could keep out of the actual killing. Although Shale had a lot to be said for him, Ralph did not often feel like saying it. Manse was radiantly uneducated but clever, powerful, strong, and, in a kind of partnership with Ember, drew half the business profits, say around £600,000 a year, net and gross. But suddenly the substances market had grown unstable, and the profits might shrink – were already shrinking. It would be a harsh and yet comfortable idea to get rid of Manse, yes, despite years of entirely unbloody acquaintanceship. Ralph had thought of it in the past, naturally, but the need now could be more pressing. Had Denzil arrived in the custom-made, glorious kit to put a very private scheme to Ember, not something for the phone or e-mail? He'd want to see exactly which ear his ideas were going into, and only one.

'It must be a real treat for you, Ralph, to have her back like permanently. Did you decide it in a hurry – like for a reason? I mean, I don't think I heard you were bringing her. At this juncture.'

'I keep matters under review,' Ember replied.

'Well, yes,' Lake said. 'And fees a real bourgeois packet, I expect.'

'Stages in her upbringing,' Ember said. He turned from Lake. 'Denzil is Mr Shane's driver and that sort of thing,' he told Venetia.

'For now,' Denzil said. Ember really noted that. He knew he was meant to note that. Some men took an extra pair of trousers with a custom-made suit. Denzil took jauntiness. It might be only mouth. It might signify he had a decent scheme for Shale's end, the sparky, treacherous sod.

Potentialities. Denzil was probably nowhere near Manse for brain and the higher ruthlessness. In a wobbly and plunging commercial context, it would be easier for Ralph to cope with Denzil than with Shale – control him. Control him for a time. Eventually, it should be feasible to wipe out Denzil, of course, and move towards a fine monopoly, all businessmen's happiest wish, whether selling double glazing or drugs. To wipe out Manse would be much more difficult, and even to think of it could send Ralph into one of his gravest panics. But if Denzil believed he could do it solo, Ember would not protest more than formally. Boardroom strategies in whatever kind of commerce could be harsh. No partnership went on eternally. There would still be Sashaying Vernon and a few other smaller firms, but the elimination of Shale and, or Denzil was a terrific, heartening prospect. Ferdy Dubal had already been sweetly taken out.*

'Which?' Venetia asked.

'Which what?' Ember replied.

'You said Denzil is Mr Shale's driver and that sort of thing. Which sort of thing?'

'General.'

'I expect he trusts you, because of closeness, Denzil,' Venetia said.

'A Jag mainly,' Lake replied.

'Oh, I love them.'

'Maybe Ven could come for a spin one day, Ralphy – I mean after seeing only them Frog cars for so long, poor duck.'

Ember loathed racist terms such as Frog, and loathed being called Ralphy, especially by a coarse twat like Denzil. People said Ralphy to make out he was slight and manageable. But if someone meant to take a drinking spot like the Monty in Shield Terrace, and jack it up to true, London gentleman's club standard, he deserved to be called better than Ralphy, like someone's retarded cousin.

'And was there trouble out there, Venetia?' Lake asked.

'What trouble?'

'So dad comes out in a rush and brings you home. Like a rescue.'

'This is a stage in Venetia's upbringing, that's all.'

'What trouble?' Venetia asked.

* The Girl with the Long Back

23

'A school out there, known about, non-vigilant – it could be targeted,' Lake replied.

'*Was* there trouble, dad?'

'What trouble, sweetheart?' Ember replied.

'Anxieties. Reasonable,' Lake said.

'A stage,' Ember said. 'We have the whole education for both our daughters mapped.'

'I'd certainly like to be concerned with looking after Venetia here,' Lake said.

'Looking after? How do you mean, Denzil?' Venetia asked.

'Not at all necessary, thank you,' Ember said.

'Have you explained everything to me, dad?'

'What about?'

'Bringing me back like that, like out of the blue.'

'Not out of the blue. A stage.'

'What does it mean? I did wonder a bit,' Venetia replied, 'but when Denzil asks, too, well, I don't know the answer. I realize it now.'

Why this slob should not be here, should not ever be here, but especially not when Venetia was. 'It's natural for you to wonder, dear,' Ember declared, gently touching her arm. 'But your mother and I had come to feel the French side of matters might be exhausted and it was time to go Brit again, as to education. There's a wonderful academic reputation here, after all – say, Oxford, reading their essays to each other with sharp but constructive comments and Aberystwyth for Prince Charles to learn Welsh.'

'What trouble, dad?'

'No trouble. Strategy. We'd always intended to bring you back about now.'

'Have there been changes here? Is this what scared you?'

'That would be an odd decision, wouldn't it – trouble here, so I bring you back to it? Scared? Would you say, Venetia, that I'm easy to scare – especially when there's nothing to scare *anyone*? No – these were stages.'

'Disturb you, then,' Venetia said.

'What changes?' Ember replied.

24

'For instance, if Mr Iles has gone. El Supremo-Cop.'

'No, Mr Iles is still here, though I don't see how he signifies,' Ember said.

'Or if he's not so high and mighty and helpful now,' Venetia replied.

'You're quick,' Lake said. 'Only back a week, but you can pick up the signs, Ven.'

'Not Ven,' Ember said. 'What signs?'

'A necktie like Denzil's, dad – like interesting but not too loud – you ought to get a tie like that for Monty members. They could buy it. Fathers used to come over to visit girls at school and they would have a tie from their London club on, like watery or clashing colours but genuine.' She went closer to Lake and drew his tie out gradually from under the top button of the jacket at full length, really handling it. Venetia was his prized daughter, but Ember had to think this somehow unmaidenly. 'Then if people from the Monty who didn't know each other met in some bar in say Madrid or the River Plate they'd joyfully cry out greetings, "You, too, are from Ralph Ember's esteemed Monty! But what a brilliant coincidence!"'

You could see they did Drama in the convents. As a matter of fact, Ember had frequently thought of a membership tie for the Monty, but not as the Monty was during this intermediary, depressed time: maybe when he had replaced all the villain element and dross and their women with quality folk, like managing directors, major estate agents, bank personnel, local TV presenters. He meant to reshape the Monty, either on the model of the Garrick, mainly for media people, lawyers and theatre folk, or the Athenaeum, which had a more scholarly and industry side. He often studied the list of London club names in Whitaker's Almanack. He loved them, and there were others besides those two to aim at – the Beefsteak, the Carlton, Chelsea Arts. The tie Denzil had on was not bad for someone with no class like Denzil, mostly blue with small silver motifs of some totally unlewd sort, but Ralph would be designing his own club tie, thank you, once the transformation began. It didn't delight him to imagine

25

the kind of lost items who might be in a bar in Madrid or the River Plate proclaiming themselves part of the Monty.

Ember's wife came in while Venetia was finger-jobbing the tie like that and he saw Margaret did not like it. She would probably be wondering, as Ember wondered himself, whether those French schools had done anything at all to get Venetia's surges less bubbly, and give her some intelligent caginess for when men were about, or men like Denzil, anyway. Margaret would drive Venetia home to Low Pastures and said it was time to leave – really said it was time to leave, like a rabbit punch on Venetia. But Venetia took her time stuffing the tie back under Denzil's jacket, sort of pretending to struggle with it as if it had veins and a busy life, also giving his chest some hand contact, no question. Teeth like that, his age, the bathmat skin – these didn't seem to matter to Venetia. Ember would have hoped she'd been forced to look at pictures of Denzil-type men as aversion therapy in the convents.

'This is a girl with spirit, Ralphy,' he said, when Margaret and Venetia had gone.

'I treasure her and her sister.'

'This I can understand, oh, definitely.'

'One sees an assured, rewarding and wholly self-satisfying future for them, perhaps in the academic world or surgery. Not media. Media's become a cesspit these days, by all accounts. As you'll know, you can get women surgeons now and nobody says any longer they lack physical strength for the chopping.'

'I wouldn't be the one to say it, Ralphy, I'm sure of that. Haven't I been thinking about careers myself?'

'Oh, that right?'

'Well, forty-two, still a chauffeur and baggage man et cetera. No great picture, is it?'

So, Ember's forecast was right. It didn't surprise him. 'Forty-two's probably an age when many wonder whether they are truly realizing themselves in their occupation,' he replied. 'A sort of last chance before old age and various palsies.'

26

'You got it at forty-two as well?'

'In a way, you're lucky, Denzil. Your face-flesh made you look old when quite young. Now, it's just that the figures are adjusting.' Although Ember did not want people from the substance trade and its enmeshments inside his club, occasionally they would ignore him and arrive like this. He always took them to a special table that he knew as fact was not bugged. Weekly, he had all the area around it electronically swept, and maybe more than weekly if those two Hun police, Harpur and Iles, had been in, showing too much interest, probably surveying the place for where *their* fucking experts could plant.

This table was just beneath a framed, blow-up photograph of Monty members setting out on that Paris excursion which, to be truthful, Ember regretted now, although this pre-journey picture showed only bright anticipation and jolly club comradeship. During the trip, Caspar Nottage and Bespoke Vincent kidnapped a tart for thirty-six hours and fractured the arm of a pimp who came looking for her. Caspar had his neck badly clawed by the woman and the pimp broke Bespoke's nose. Happily, nobody had wanted to bring the French police in. Since then, Ember refused to endorse Monty trips abroad or in this country. Ralph knew that kind of incident clearly did not harmonize with his wish to upgrade the Monty to Athenaeum level. The excursion photograph must be the most frequently removed picture worldwide, because of the mike searches. It was the main reason he always chose this table for confidential talks. If the police did try eavesdropping they'd go for the easiest place to hide a mike. That's how they were.

He brought a bottle of Kressmann armagnac with its homely black label and a couple of glasses and sat down with Lake. People would see them, of course, and wonder. But as soon as Denzil entered the club and began talking to Venetia and Ralph he must have been spotted by one of the few afternoon customers and the buzz would be around. Why Ember tried to keep trade associates out of the Monty. Useless to aim for secrecy now and Ralph had led to the conference table as soon as Margaret and Venetia left.

'So did you think Manse might send a task force over to pick up Ven and lock her away?' Denzil said. 'Is that the sort of partner you want, Ralphy?'

'Certain formalities – could we observe them? Her name's Venetia and mine is Ralph or Ember, not Ralphy. How would you wish me to address *you* – Denzil or Lake?'

'If Manse had something like that planned, he might tell me, he might not. He does things his own shady fucking way. He might know I'd object – using a kid like that. Sickening. I think of Lorraine Sambrook, obviously – I mean, as well as Curly and his live-in.'

'As a matter of fact, Venetia had stayed rather longer in France than we'd originally planned, owing to uncertainties about private education in this country under Blair. But I decided he's got it pretty well right – jabber about improved education for everyone, the way they have to, but make sure your own kids are fixed up nicely, anyway.'

'And moving her from Poitiers to Bordeaux – oh, Ralph Ember is quick.'

'To get a range of academic influences for her, you know.'

'Well, anyone can see she's really benefited from it, Ralphy. Ralph. That's top class scent she got on, but moderate, no heavy campaign. Or, to be fair, I suppose not just Manse might've wanted to get her so he could squeeze you, but other trade eminences. That Ferdy Dubal, for instance, dead now, yes, but dangerous before being found an exit. Or Sashaying Vern.'

'I like the suit,' Ember replied. 'Gives you solemnity.'

'So, how you coping, Ralph? I mean, apart from getting your daughter safe from maybe Manse?'

This prick talked as if already someone. *How you coping?* It was like equal to equal, or even high to low. Had things happened in Shale's firm that Ember didn't know – not deaths yet, obviously, he'd have heard, but power and money adjustments? The suit would cost a thousand plus and his black lace-ups could be Charles Laity. The point about the suit was it undoubtedly looked made for him, not hand-me-down, which would need measuring up and fittings, a planned gesture over at least weeks, no impulse only. It must have been deeply nauseating for the tailor, forced to contact Lake's body like that more than once. True, Venetia did not seem to mind it. The need to put up with French food might have helped her develop a tough stomach, though this had certainly not been envisaged by Margaret and Ralph.

'Like *coping*, I mean,' Lake said.

'And Manse – is he all right, getting enough of it – a girl cohabiting these days?' Ember replied. 'Lowri? Or Carmel? Or Patricia? Manse has delicacy. Never shacked up with more than one at a time.'

'Ralph, do you understand when I say "coping"?'

This was often the way with thickoes. They came up with a word they thought was really fresh and soulful and they couldn't drop it. Politicians were the worst, obviously. They'd discover 'community' or 'care' – or 'democracy', of course – and here we go . . . and go. Ember said: 'Many would think Manse is a real piece of crudity, yet these girls keep coming back when whistled for even if they're with someone else, and it can't be just the gems and dresses and living for a while with whitebait and truffles in an ex-rectory.'

'A new Chief Constable,' Lake said.

'This could have plus aspects – as well as some uncertainties, admittedly.'

'Fucking enlightened,' Lake replied.

'The style of some of the younger ones.'

'That's what they fucking call it, "enlightened", the Press and all that,' Lake said.

'The days have disappeared when Chief Constables were retired army officers, possibly out of touch with trends. These people like to feel they're on the cusp.'

'I heard of them – cusps,' Lake replied.

'Leaders – that's where they like to be.'

'In the cusp?'

'On it,' Ember said. 'Or call it the cutting edge.'

'On the cutting edge?'

'At it.' You put up with this kind of conversation now and then in case a born jerk like Denzil really had something to get out, eventually, something helpful and possibly destructive. It was only very early evening, not many folk in the club yet, so Ember could give him a while. Later tonight, there was a party for Sashaying Vernon's bail, and Ralph must be available then to make sure the champagne kept pace and the vol-au-vents, and in case of fights and, or careless puking. In his way, Denzil looked not too bad. You could get faces like his in sepia photographs of serfs illustrating the history of the camera – a kind of blunt and possibly unevil ordinariness to them, even if a bit aslant. He drank the Kressmann in quite reasonable sips, not tipping it down. It was still terrible to think of him bodily close to Venetia as happened earlier and her enthusiasm, but his eyebrows seemed intelligently trimmed and he didn't gape.

'Where does enlightened leave us, Ralph?'

'Who?'

'I know you've thought of it. You was at the college for a while.'

'Mature student. I've put my degree on hold because of business pressures – the club and so on.'

'You been taught to see the total picture.'

'Factors. I try to weigh all of them.'

'This is an art, Ralph.'

'A procedure. A drill.'

'You been wondering, yes?'

'What?'

'Why I'm here – like solo.'

'Well, I –'

'You don't like trade folk in the club, do you?'

'Well, I –'

'People come sniffing – wanting your facilities, the Monty facilities, for trade, but you won't have it, will you,

Ralph? So you don't ask people like that here whatsoever. All right, let's say like me.'

'There's different aspects to life, many various aspects, all valid,' Ember replied.

'What is this – what I got to ask – what we all got to ask – is, What is this?'

'What?' Ember said.

'Enlightened.'

'Enlightened?'

'What are they getting at?'

'A media word. One of their labels,' Ember replied.

'Yeah, but signifying?'

'Well, I –'

'This is just a Chief turning trendy, Ralph. He's picked up the present mood. What he *thinks* is the present mood.'

'There's probably more to it than –'

'All right, you say cusp. Cusps are fine, but me, I say trendy. Big peaked hat with all the gold on and kid gloves and he still tells the country and the fucking world, "Maybe the substances laws are too hard. Maybe some loosening up is required."' Lake put on what the sod thought was a Command Suite voice, but it still sounded like Denzil, Denzil with his balls in a crusher. Ember would drink to that. Lake was like the Saul-Paul incident on the road to Damascus. He had become someone new – the suit, the tie, the theory spiel, the Monty visit, the fucking gross, cut-across interruptions, like Prince Philip. 'This is an officer saying it, Ralph, not some Right Honourable polony in the House of Commons or a *Guardian* dreamer. He's heard people like that say it or write it, so he thinks he'll swim with them – thinks he'll look like a mind. You know what I mean when I say "a mind"? Like intellectual. Some police don't want to be regarded as just big boots and a Heckler and Koch.'

'I don't believe –'

'Ralph, Ralph, look what happened to Ecstasy. Four or five years ago, what did a tablet go for – £10? More? Now? We're doing one-for-one on the street, got to. By one-for-one, what do I mean? One tablet, one sterling pound. There's livelihoods slipping away here, Ralph, comfort, security, proper reward, inheritances.'

'I wouldn't say that's because of the new Chief,' Ember replied. 'It's general over the country. Supplies are up.'

'So right, Ralphy. What's happened to scarcity? Scarcity's fucking scarce. That's what helped us so beautiful, Ralphy, in them grand old days. Ralph. Remember Robert Duval in *Godfather 2*? "We were like the Holy Roman Empire," he said, meaning the Corleone family. Well, *we* were like the Holy Roman Empire, or you and Manse. Me, then, I did only odd jobs and driving, but I still felt part of it. Proud. Stuff was tough to get. We had it. You and Manse – these was firms that knew how to what's referred to as maximize – you heard of that, at all? – meaning, we could ask a price and people didn't see no option, they paid it. All right, we had a nice nod and wink from Ilesy for the sake of order, but pushing still had perils, and we could charge for risk. Danger money. Now? Now, everything is fucking *enlightened*. If the Chief and other Chiefs decide the law's too tough on the commodities, where's peril gone, Ralphy? Where's the fucking price gone? Stuff can come in like a big tide and the punters splash about in it for nearly free, nobody bothers. Ilesy's blind eye? Not needed no more because every law fucker's blind-eyeing.'

He gazed at the outing picture for half a minute, then said: 'You heard that saying at all, "In the land of the blind the one-eyed man is king"? So, in the land of blind-eyeing coke comes cheap. All substances. Substances. There's a word, Ralph. In the old days it was "illegal substances". And that's the particular business area where you and Manse and myself after a lot of thinking and weighing up decided to make our careers. We could have been anything that produced the right sort of income, but we chose the substances area. Now, it's going to be gone – the illegal side. Not the substances side – the illegal side. This is a whole way of life fucked up, Ralphy, without no consultation or consideration, nothing, and obviously no compensation. What it makes me think of is under Thatcher no more coal mining. A total good industry shut, and who cares about all the men who used to get down them pits and built their villages around? This is us, Ralphy. Ralph. Scrapheaped. Scrapheaped if we let them do it.'

The club was beginning to fill up. Some early ones for Sashaying Vernon's bail occasion arrived and started getting convivial and into ballads. Ralph must be at readiness soon. As he understood things, Sashaying used a full QC in court plus sidekick to get him out. This was a menaces charge, not just a naughty-naughty job. The lawyers must be something. Sashaying might bring the pair for a drink-up before they went back to London and it would be important Ember met them so they could sense at once from his easy poise that, although the Monty might look only two steps up from a shit heap now, there was brilliant potentiality here powered by unflagging vision. He hated the Monty to look cheap: big-voiced barristers having a shudder about it first class on the train, as if they'd just been to secret badger baiting. Oh, God, he didn't want fights and knives tonight. Back in London these legal voices could talk about his club in spots where influence counted, mentioning its possible future resemblances to the Athenaeum.

Lake said: 'To long and short it, Ralph, takings are going to sink and sink.'

'Oh, I think you're –'

'And when the money gets short this is when the fighting starts, yes? Starving rats, you throw them a bit of food and they'll kill each other for it. I'm not saying you're a rat, obviously, Ralph, it's like to compare it, that's all. What do you call the behaviour of someone who'd send to a lovely school in France to grab your fine and much treasured daughter? That's the actions of an animal. No different from what happened to Curly and the other two. Why I came to see you, Ralph. Do I want to be tied to someone who thinks like that? Do you? And now, no Iles to get matters arranged and neat, because his power's gone. The new Chief has taken it from him and in any case Ilesy's

33

way of looking at things is not his special way no more – everyone's doing it.'

'This reminds me of *Leviathan*, as a matter of fact,' Ember replied, nodding a couple of times to confirm it.

'That don't surprise me a bit.'

Mature students at the university had been given a Foundation Year when starting their degrees and Ralph enjoyed the Introduction to Philosophy lectures, especially works from the seventeenth century. 'This was a book by Thomas Hobbes. He thought men were so alike and so competitive they'd destroy one another unless controlled by a government.'

'Did he mention the drugs firms and all this fucking enlightened – making the stuff too easy to get?' Lake asked.

'Well, hardly, Denz. We're talking about a book –'

'If he came down and had a look at this realm in the new conditions he must have seen there's not enough no longer for a lot of firms. "Permissiveness". That's another word they use, like "enlightened". Permissiveness has destroyed a lovely business structure, Ralph. This could be why the one you mentioned wrote the book, especially if he knew what's happened to Iles.'

'I don't think –'

'Yes, why I'm here.'

'What?' Ember replied.

'One firm eventually.'

'Yes, but I don't see –'

'If I'm here it shows which firm I want it to be, doesn't it,' Lake said. 'You at the top, Ralph, clearly, with one good, loyal first mate, a loyal first mate who will never allow any hell-brute get near your fine daughter. Because I'd always be very close with my body, to shield her.'

'But Manse is never going to –'

'We cut out all these middle people with their fucking BMWs to run and gold medallions. Big saving – what they been getting, plus what they skim.'

'Manse will –'

Lake finished his armagnac and stood. 'So, sounds on

34

the right lines, Ralphy? Have I got your . . . your like OK for developments? Developments you can leave to me.'

'Developments meaning that you'll –'

'Developments. I enjoyed our talk, Ralphy. Ralph. And meeting your wife plus Venetia also. This is a really noticeable girl, and a true plus for you.'

Ember could see Denzil believed he already had a bigged-up stature, something more than what the suit gave. Probably he thought he was not just *entitled* to have Venetia stroke his tie, he believed he gave her a treat by it, and by letting her near enough to smell her scent. If Ember went with Lake's business plan, Denzil might grow bigger and bigger still, fruitier and fruitier. Venetia would get responsive about this, no question. Responsiveness came damn easily to her. Venetia could respond before there was anything to respond *to*. She would love it if Lake had a Jaguar of his own. Ember ran good cars – Saabs and so on – and through being brought up like that, before France, Venetia would expect a man to own quite a vehicle. Probably she thought Denzil Lake looked utterly suitable to have a Jaguar of his own. This was the silly, generous way kids could be. Ralph did not want her in a Jaguar with him or in anywhere else with him.

But on the other side, he had been thrilled by Denzil's scheme. Amazing to hear a nonentity do a price analysis like that, even if he couldn't always manage the actual grammar and sentences right. Because of Venetia, Ember feared building Lake more sizeable. But he approved the kind of operation Denzil proposed, with Denzil handling all its terrifying side, such as removal of Manse. Although in many ways, Manse could be a lovely chap, possibly he had to go. Yet if Denzil succeeded with that he'd be a major item and ungovernable. So would Venetia be ungovernable. God, but couldn't swinish dilemmas hit a man as business leader and parent?

Just after Denzil left, Sashaying Vernon turned up smile-rich and looking very bailed, wearing a sort of beige siren suit. 'Ralph Ember,' he called, 'please meet my accomplished and devoted briefs, Rosie and Matthew.' He put an arm around Ember's shoulders. 'Here's Ralph, the soul of the Monty and custodian of all our hopes.'

'That's the only kind of custodian you want familiarity with, Vernon,' Rosie QC said.

Ember said: 'One has in mind the gradual evolvement of this centre on the model of certain London clubs which I'm sure you're familiar with.'

'Some won't have me or any woman as members,' Rosie QC said.

'Absurd,' Ember replied. 'Well, those will not be the model, I assure you.'

'Ralph's well up with all forward-looking movements,' Sashaying Vernon remarked warmly, and not piss-taking, as far as Ember could make out, though Vern had that kind of voice which you could never be sure about – bloody poised, the poised sod, jail-familiar or not. 'When you see a letter in the Press signed Ralph W. Ember on environmental and anti-pollution matters you know it will be strong, and *so* committed,' he said.

'A duty, nothing more than that,' Ember replied. 'A basic vigilance.' He always enjoyed talking to people like Rosie QC and Matthew. They had that metropolitan bounce and gab to them, smelled of the highest quality traffic congestion – Bentleys and coupé Mercedes. They delighted in good topics, the same as Ralph. Her clothes were fucking awful, courtroom clothes and then worse, but there must have been a time far back – say the late 1970s – when she looked something. Not something much even then. Something, though. A conversation with Rosie and Matthew sang and had big differences from a conversation with Denzil, and even with Sashaying Vernon on his own. This was Ralph's present agony, though, wasn't it? He realized he wouldn't ever meet such folk as Rosie and Matthew except through Vernon, or similar.

And wasn't Denzil crucial to Ember's status and fine intentions, also? When Ralph promised to improve the Monty, he realized this rebirth depended on large, steady investment in the club of money gained via his other commercial side, the substances trade. Denzil came from that area of his life, didn't he? Where else? Not the Baptist College. But substances profits had already started to fall, due unquestionably to the disgusting change of attitude by law makers and their police slobs, especially their local police slobs, Harpur and Iles. No wonder Denzil kept on asking in his crude, worrying way what 'enlightened' meant. This damn modish enlightenment in the authorities brought lousy, darkest shadows for Ralph. If last quarter's showing was typical of the new, degrading, nearly free-for-all conditions, he reckoned he'd be right down to not much over £350,000 this year net and gross. The only way to restore proper income tone might be a cuddling up to Denzil, provided, that is, naturally, Denzil managed to do Manse first. God, Denzil could not expect proximity unless he earned it. This meant the grand future of the Monty might depend on a born bit of famous crud like Lake. Irony, irony – no other word.

Ember kept the mind arguments going still. He could see at least two reasons for rejecting Denzil, or for telling Manse on the quiet what Denzil planned – result, Denzil dead. First, Venetia, who would be more impressed by him the higher he seemed to go in that fucking suit and tie, if he did. Second came the sacred nature of Ember's vision for the Monty and his heartfelt drive to make the club clean and distinguished worldwide.

Yes . . . yes . . . but, on the other hand, a cash drop from £600,000 to just over half that, and possibly down even more, was bound to trouble Ralph, almost to the point of despair and one of his deepest panics. As a prominent figure, Ember had certainly met and resolved appalling conundrums. This was the worst ever, though: he needed people like Denzil now, so he and the Monty could eventually soar away for ever . . . from people like Denzil. Yes, irony, irony, by the fucking bucketful. Obviously, he saw the enforced nature of this relationship as almost identical to that between Britain and Russia in 1941, two nations always suspicious of each other, yet joining to fight Hitler.

'If one is in a position of some minor eminence in a town

37

– and I'd definitely not put it as beyond minor – but this being so, one does feel an obligation to look at general civic problems and offer suggestions through the public sheets,' Ralph told Rosie. When barristers became QCs it was called 'taking silk', but Rosie seemed to have gone for cast-off shoddy.

Chapter Three

Oh, God, it seemed Iles was turning into the old Chief, Mark Lane. Iles had helped destroy him – in fact destroyed him more or less on his own, first harrying Lane towards breakdown and then ensuring his promotion to something eminent and harmless and far away. Yet, now, Iles began to act like Lane pre-collapse, a kind of nostalgia for Lane's mist and fine simplicities. Harpur could understand it – definitely had a theory on why it would happen – but he still felt troubled.

For instance, during the combined funerals of Curly Sambrook and his daughter, Lorraine, Iles behaved exactly as Lane would have – total self-effacement and patent, huge grief: absolutely no shouting, or attempts to get into the pulpit and run things, or fist attacks on the vicar and, or other members of the congregation. Generally, Harpur loathed partnering Iles at crime victim funerals in case a scrap started. The ACC was famed for funerals. At several he'd tried to take over all or at least most of the service because he thought the minister was not getting to the essentials, and, obviously, Harpur had feared now the extra stress on him of paired deaths, one a child. Although Iles's spasms would not invariably mean violence, sometimes they did, and Harpur regarded it as poor that he must be constantly ready to arm lock a very senior officer in a place of worship among floral tributes.

But nothing anywhere near this occurred at the solemnities for Curly and Lorraine. The ACC sat alongside Harpur well back in the nave, head lowered, shoulders hunched around quiet agony, obviously ashamed that these deaths could occur on a police ground where he had big rank and big responsibility. It was the identical guilt Lane would have shown if still Chief. Vile killings on the manor had always devastated him, made Lane doubt his own fitness for the post, his own commitment, his endorsement by God as Number One. Iles sang the hymns with fine restraint, absolutely unlike the Now-hear-this tannoy on American aircraft carriers, his funeral tone generally.

And then another dismaying resemblance to Lane. Iles said he wanted a look inside the gutted Sambrook house. 'Yes, I need it, Col. A pull I'm aware constantly of.' This could have nothing to do with detection. Fire teams and Harpur's people under Francis Garland had already made their searches, trying to fix the outbreak's cause and find anything that said what made Curly a target. Harpur put a heavy-duty jemmy, a hammer, some six-inch nails and a couple of flashlights in the old, anon car he had from the police pool and drove Iles to the Ernest Bevin. The ACC wore dark dungarees and a thick, navy wool hat. Subfuscness – Iles tonight could not be more that. Impossible to think of him in that boulevardier bomber jacket and crimson scarf. Good. Brilliant. Get the sod deglamorized. Come and view him now, Hazel – respectably, tamely sad, Laned, cowed, commonplace, undangerous. Even his teeth looked subfusc.

Yes, good in that way – that one, definitely important way. But Harpur had other reactions, too. Didn't it unnerve him to see Iles like this? Iles should be Iles, eternally Iles, moving so easily in that select style of his between genius and arrant evil, not some crushed, decently behaved figure wearing artisan gear, his ferocious brain neutered. This really might be the onset of chaos, comparable with President Tito's death and the Yugoslavia mess after. Yes, of course, Harpur could make a guess at what was happening. Under the old Chief, Iles had been able to behave destructively, loutishly, now and then or oftener, because, despite it all, he *was* still under the old Chief. Iles knew that the system endured, intact, blessed, potentially effective, as long as Lane had office. And Iles needed this system, was part of this system, his jolly subversiveness a feature of it, or a feint. He had to have something to subvert, required a Chief, however weak. To kick against authority meant authority, leadership, stability did exist, would even prevail. Its rod and its staff, they comforted him. Iles thrived in a cocoon. Hierarchy he despised and adored. He was a for-ever second string and knew it.

But now, under Lane's successor, subversion became naff. All Iles's views on tolerance towards the big drugs boys like Ember and Manse Shale were suddenly OK, not maverick at all. This scared the ACC, gave him a terrifying dose of limbo. He felt the command chain had annulled itself, the structure would collapse, or had already. Yes, chaos. Harpur was once a Sunday School lad and kept vaguely in his subconscious New Testament verses listing signs of imminent apocalypse: 'When ye shall see such things come to pass, look up . . .' Perhaps Iles had begun to see such things and was looking up. Now, astoundingly, he longed to restore Mark Lane and his clear, old values – values the ACC had previously loved to piss on. But it was impossible to restore Lane, so Iles would do the Lane job himself. He wanted Lane's mantle, the way Elisha succeeded Elijah – Old Testament, this time. As Iles saw it, the alternative was final calamity. Harpur decided he would get down to the city's drug-dealing quarter around Valencia Esplanade and look for inklings of catastrophic change – change destined to get unstoppably worse, if Iles had things right. Iles generally did. Harpur grasped things better if he saw them on the street. He'd go to the Valencia as soon as he could ditch Iles.

And six months later, Harpur would find it hard – impossible – to explain why he happened to be in the right part of the district at exactly the time to watch the murderous gun battle there that night. He felt it would seem absurd and far-fetched to tell the court he wanted to check whether the Assistant Chief Constable's anxieties and sensitivities were justified and chaos had arrived –

although the shootings could be seen as proof it had. When the trial eventually began after that clash, Harpur would be up in the box early as main prosecution witness to describe the four killings. In the defence counsel's cross-examination questions then came the repeated suggestion – only the suggestion, but certainly present, and repeated – the repeated suggestion that Harpur knew more about the events of that night than he had disclosed: that he might somehow be an implicated party, not a spectator on the spot by fluke. Few defence counsel believed in police fluke.

Now, as they entered the Ernest Bevin, en route to Curly's, the Assistant Chief said: 'I seek fullness, Col.'
    'Which species of fullness might that be, sir?'
    'Of experience. I have to *know*.'
    'Know what?'
    'The gamut. I have to *feel* the setting from which Curly and his family came. Feel it, *live* it.'
    'I'm afraid this setting's not recognizable now, after the fire.'
    'I don't want to *recognize* it, you fucking jerk. I have to *feel* it, *live* it,' Iles replied.
    'Recognize, feel, live – they're different?'
    'The burning is incidental only.'
    'I'll tell Curly's woman, when she's fit to listen.'
    'A communion with their place. That's what I seek.'
    'Right, sir.'
    'Sound like bollocks?' Iles replied.
    'Of course.'
    'Haven't you done the same – broken into villains' homes secretly, breathed their surroundings, absorbed ambience and motivation?'
    'How do you know that, you sod?' Harpur said.
    'I *feel* you're the kind who would.'
    'You're into feelings all of a sudden, aren't you? Been reading Barbara Cartland again?'
    This trip was the sort Lane used to insist on now and then. He would abruptly decide a particular criminal act

42

meant vastly more than itself – that it symbolized potential failure of order not merely here, but spreading out from his patch to become national, perhaps international, possibly cosmic. Galloping out. The site of the offence then acquired a dark, terminal significance, and Lane's sense of duty would force him to face up and make a personal pilgrimage. He'd *feel* fated. Harpur saw it was like that now with Iles. For him, perhaps Curly's death and the child's and this house shell signalled the beginning of that disintegration. Like Lane, he had to come and do a defeated headbow *in situ*. Iles would make sure his profile got the right showing while he did it and try to minimize his Adam's apple.

As quietly as he could, Harpur levered off some boarding at the rear of the house and they climbed in. Harpur left the jemmy and the hammer and nails outside. The floor of this room still had small pools from fire hoses. They used a flashlight each. Charred furniture and carpet remains were piled in one corner. Several wisps of undestroyed green or grey wallpaper hung near a bit of surviving, blackened picture rail. The stink of ash held Harpur like a professional noose. Iles appeared to breathe it in greedily, gulping and sucking with grandiose noise, as if this were part of the atmospherics he craved – as if he didn't deserve decent air any more, only the reek of a disaster he'd sponsored by idiocy or doziness. Penance. Theatricals?

'This would be their sitting room, I expect, Col. He'd come back here with his bits of street money behaving like the big, successful dad. A girl's dad – he's always the tops in her view, isn't he? Ah, daughters. We're lucky like that, you and I.'

'They were all in bed, of course,' Harpur replied. 'Curly tried to get to the child. That's what killed him.'

Iles walked across the small room and back. Glass crackled softly, respectfully under his stupendous shoes. 'Would *my* daughter think I'm tops if she knew I'd let Curly's daughter get it like that, Col?'

'I don't think you –'

43

'Look at this room, Harpur.'

'Not good now, obviously, but after a fire which room anywhere would be fit to –'

'The pokiness, fire or not. What does it say, Col?'

'Council building of this period was pretty basic and –'

'When minor, shit-head, municipal house people like Curly are hit we're into the absolutely worst trouble, Col. Everyone can understand princes of the game warring and killing. Fortunes to be had. But the money Curly handled would be piffling. Enough to bring fire? Only if we're already into utter decomposition. Even supposing he grassed it would be little league grassing. At his level, he wouldn't know much. Enough to bring fire? Only if we're already into utter decomposition.' He walked to a wall and held the beam of the flashlight up close. 'I'd say a picture hung here, Col. Yes, yes, a picture.' Iles turned his light on to the heap of wrecked kit, probably searching for a fragment of frame, like an art collector tipped off about good stuff in the attic. 'What sort of picture would you say, Harpur? This is what I meant by fullness. I require all the key details of their mini, council estate life. What might seem inconsequential to many is vital to me. Can you understand, I wonder?'

'Picture? Kittens, bright-eyed, pink-nosed, playing with wool in mischievous yet endearing fashion.'

'Ah. You've been to the house pre-fire on some Curly inquiries?'

'No.'

'Why do you say that then, I wonder, Col – the kittens?'

'I *feel* it.'

Iles swung the beam on to Harpur's face, like old time interrogation, and kicked some glass slivers hard at his trouser legs, aiming for wounds and possible septicaemia. 'Don't fucking take the mick with me, Harpur.' Under the wool hat, and with a little bit of undirected light, the Assistant Chief's features now looked touched by that traditional, splendid Iles malevolence, harmonizing sweetly with the background filth and devastation.

44

Christ, such a comfort to hear Iles snarl. Welcome back. Harpur had provoked him for this. It would be dereliction to let decency drag the ACC irrecoverably down. 'How do you mean, sir, "take the mick"?' he replied. 'Would I take the mick in such a tragic setting?'

'I think an enlargement of a family holiday snap in Looe or Algeciras. Now, though, that family is as good as gone, obliterated. I want the items who did this to them, Col.'

'Garland's working on it, with the drugs squad people.'

'All right, Curly was negligible, but this is a family destroyed. I revere the concept of family, Col.'

Harpur felt like saying, *Right, so revere mine and fucking well lay off Hazel, will you?* But he feared this would only nudge Iles into spit-lipped tit-for-tat bitterness about Sarah and him again. 'The concept of family and yourself are for ever linked in many minds, sir, and so justifiably.'

'At Staff College I was known as "Kindred Desmond".'

'I've heard all sorts of names for you, sir, as people try to sum up the youness of you.'

'Things are slipping away from us, Harpur.'

'I believe we –'

'And would you please tell the court whether it is customary for you, a Detective Chief Superintendent, not a patrolling constable – is it customary, normal for you, Detective Chief Superintendent, to be strolling an area of the city, without any apparent purpose, at 1.40 in the morning?'

'Walking, not strolling.'

'Is it customary for you, Detective Chief Superintendent, to walk an area of the city, without any apparent purpose, at 1.40 in the morning?'

'Not customary, not unusual. I like to see at first hand the ground we police.'

'In the middle of the night, Detective Chief Superintendent?'

'In the middle of the night the Valencia district is at its most interesting and might require most policing.'

*   *   *

'I hope I'm not one arrogantly to claim I'm totally, continuously sane, Col,' the Assistant Chief said, pacing the
torched room. He took the beam off Harpur and let it
slowly move around.

'I'd certainly remember if I'd ever heard you argue that,
sir. It would stand out. Or if anyone else did.'

'But the madness is come-and-go only. Extremely come-
and-go.'

'I believe people who know you would never dispute
this, sir. Hardly any. Almost definitely. And the point is,
nearly everyone can tell when the madness has come and
when it's gone. Many see quite a difference in you between
the times you're mad and those when you're not. I believe
you have a right to boast of this, mention it in your CV.'

'Madness is entirely unlikely to reach my daughter
genes-wise.'

'Absolutely. Just as you, when mad or sane, are utterly
unlikely to reach *my* daughter, sir.'

'Do you think she'll be all right, Col?'

'Who?'

'My daughter, Fanny.'

'In what way?' Harpur replied.

'Mentally. I don't want her with a shaky mind because
of me.'

'Might get her to be Assistant Chief,' Harpur said.

'Whenever I sense a spasm coming I do fight it.'

'This is another of your pluses, sir.'

'I have a procedure.'

'That right?'

'I'll repeat old popular song titles to myself – "She Was
Only A Bird In A Gilded Cage", "When The Red, Red
Robin Comes Bob, Bob, Bobbing Along".'

'I gather psychiatrists dish out a list of these for use by
patients at home,' Harpur replied.

'Daughters are quite a thing, Col. King Lear was so
right, wasn't he?'

'Do you want to see upstairs?' Harpur replied.

'Where they found the child? No, I won't go there. No.
No.' The wet walls produced a gentle, muted echo, so

46

Harpur heard six aghast refusals. He was always confused by surges of humanity in the ACC.

'We ought to leave, before someone gets a vigilante group together and beats shit out of us as vandals.'

Iles pondered. 'And *are* we that, Col? I mean, vandals in the general sense.'

Oh, Jesus.

Iles said: 'Destroyers of order, not its preservers.'

'The wool hat was intelligent, sir,' Harpur replied. 'There's a dankness here.'

'I think of Lear quite a bit lately, Col.'

'Probably very clever of you not to go upstairs. We'd be trapped if a mob did come.'

'"Oh, let me not be mad,"' Iles said. He seemed to sob.

'Sir, I wouldn't, if it was up to me. But –'

'Lear.'

Could you tell us, please, Detective Chief Superintendent, how you spent the earlier part of that evening and night?'

And, of course, at the Valencia trial Harpur could but didn't want to. He gave it to the court, though, in an adjusted version. After all, there were one or two folk who might come forward and say how Harpur and Iles spent the earlier part of that evening and night. 'With the Assistant Chief Constable, I visited the home of Mr Gerald Sambrook on the Ernest Bevin estate.'

'The burned house?'

'Yes.'

'Why?'

'To check it was secure.'

'Does this require an Assistant Chief Constable and a Detective Chief Superintendent, Detective Chief Superintendent?'

'This was a routine visit.'

'A routine visit involving an Assistant Chief Constable and a Detective Chief Superintendent, Detective Chief Superintendent?'

'This was a sensitive site.'

* * *

47

Harpur said: 'The hammering when I replace the boards could bring people. Will you keep an eye, sir? They'd probably recognize me and even you, but that wouldn't help with safety, would it?'

'Safety? Is this our only consideration now, then? Mere self-preservation? Is it, is it, Col?'

'One consideration.'

'Shall I tell you what I learned in that house?' the ACC said. They were outside.

'Cheap furniture burns best.' Harpur started to nail the boards back. He was still working when he realized Iles had turned away.

'Hello there,' the ACC said pleasantly. 'Who are you?'

The house was on a corner and a boy of fourteen or fifteen had walked down the drive from the street into the back garden and now stood watching them. Harpur and Iles had taken the same route earlier.

'We're the people who repair things,' the Assistant Chief said. 'You're out late, aren't you?'

'Which people?' the boy asked.

'Who repair things,' Iles said.

'Being sent by?'

'No, just to repair things,' Iles said. 'These boards. They get loose. The weather.'

'So what about the jemmy?' the boy replied, pointing to where it lay near Harpur's feet.

'You know that word, do you?' Iles said.

'Why shouldn't I?' He was close-cropped, thin, long-faced, in three-quarter length loose khaki shorts and a beige zip-up fleece one size or more too big. He wore blue plimsolls. He needed a skateboard. Harpur had stopped hammering while they talked but resumed now. The boy did not move. Harpur finished. The boy said: 'Sashaying sent you?'

'Do you live close?' Iles asked. 'You saw the lights, did you? Smart.'

'Why Sashaying?' Harpur said.

'Sashaying's out now,' the boy replied.

'That right?' Harpur said.

'You knew, did you?' the boy asked. 'Everyone knows. A party at Panicking Ralphy's dump, the Monty. Only bail. Maybe he'll go down. But even when he was inside Sashaying could arrange some things, couldn't he? Fire. Then, when he gets out he sends you here, does he, to see the score?'

'What things could he arrange from inside?' Harpur replied.

'Sashaying's got friends, haven't he?' the boy said. 'They jump. He could pass a word.'

'You think Curly Sambrook crossed Sashaying somehow?' Harpur replied. 'How? Was Curly the competition – two small-time pushers squabbling?'

The boy looked at the ruined house. 'That's more than a squabble. Anyway, you know what it was about, if Sashaying sent you to find the score.'

'What score?' Iles asked.

'Make sure the house is clean. No evidence,' the boy said. 'But isn't it too late?'

'What's your name, laddie?' Iles asked.

'Or are you police?' the boy said. 'I mean, that fucking stupid hat. And all his questions.' He pointed at Harpur.

'What's the talk about who did it?' Harpur replied.

'Did what?' the boy said.

'The burning.'

'What do you mean, "the talk"?' the boy asked.

'You know – the talk,' Harpur replied.

'Who talks about something like that?' the boy said.

'Yes, who does?' Harpur asked.

'People don't talk about something like that, they'd be scared,' the boy said.

'Why would they be scared?' Harpur asked.

'Who?'

'The people who don't talk about it,' Harpur said.

'Chip fat,' the boy replied.

'An accident?' Harpur asked. 'They say an accident?'

'Chip fat,' the boy said.

'At three in the morning?' Harpur asked.

'That Curly – he'd be out late often. This was well

49

known. A bit of supper. He've had a few bevvies. Leaves the pan too long, the heat too high. Up she goes. Police, are you, not from Sashaying? Yeah, I think I reckernize you now on the News. I should of before. Not expecting it, a detective hammering. Not hammering nails and wood.'

'Which is your house?' Iles asked.

'And was *the house secure, Detective Chief Superintendent?'*

That boy might be somewhere around as possible witness, so the question should be answered: 'A section of boarding needed repair.'

'You attended to that?'

'Yes.'

'So, you, a Detective Chief Superintendent and an Assistant Chief Constable, had gone there with builder's equipment?'

'Basic tools.'

'Why was the house so important to you?'

'It had been the site of a serious incident.'

'But several weeks before.'

'It was still regarded as a sensitive site.'

The boy waved a hand at Curly's place. 'This is what's known as a property.'

'Well, yes,' Harpur said.

'A lot of these are properties now,' the boy said.

'Well, yes,' Harpur said.

'Know what I mean when I say a property?' the boy asked.

'Well, yes.' Harpur waved a hand at Curly's place.

'It was his. Not rent,' the boy said.

'He bought it?' Iles asked. 'A council house but he bought it?'

'Why I called it a property. Many around here are properties now. It was the government started it way back – said they could buy them. In history. Before that, only rent.'

'Mrs Thatcher,' Iles replied.

'Curly had some money, so he could get a property. He did his window cleaning round at the big houses now and then but most times there was other money coming in as well.'

'How do you know that?' Harpur replied.

'Don't ask me where from,' the boy said.

'Pushing,' Harpur said.

'This is a property, so there was bound to be other money. I expect you live in a property,' the boy said.

'*I* do,' Iles said. 'My friend's is not *really* a property. I don't know what I'd call it. But he's happy there. What he's used to.'

'Have *you* got other money coming in?' the boy asked.

'What other money?' Harpur said.

'You know – like *other* money, not just the police pay. What people say.'

'Which people?' Iles asked.

'Other money – if you been able to buy a property,' the boy replied. 'I expect yours got a garage, even double. No garage with these properties, just the drive.'

'When I say the talk around here, I mean did you hear people speak about enemies of Curly?' Harpur said.

'I know,' the boy replied. 'You been looking for *clues*, I expect. Nobody's not going to tell you nothing.'

'We meet a lot of folk like that,' Iles replied.

'Chip fat.' The boy walked away.

'Envy,' Harpur said.

'What envy?'

'House envy. People who can buy their council house are still thought snooty. The boy's heard his parents sniping at Sambrook, I should think. So, he doesn't mind speaking to us about him.' Harpur picked up the jemmy and then drove Iles to Idylls, his home in Rougemont Place. The house was dark. The ACC paused as he began to leave the car, and with a hand on the open door looked back over his shoulder and said: 'Tell me, Harpur – now, look, this isn't madness or sick curiosity – but tell me, did you ever actually fuck her here, actually *here*, at Idylls?'

'Fuck your property in your property?'

Iles started to shout, still part out of the vehicle, his body half twisted around. 'Whenever we discuss you now, do you know what she'll do? Do you, Harpur? She'll wrinkle her nose, yes, wrinkle her nose. It's distastefully. I'd say distastefully – yet amusing and attractive. And then she'll laugh at the memory of you. How do you think she'll laugh, Harpur?'

'This is a good area, sir. It's late. You'll upset the neighbours with the din. People in such a street – if they come to the bedroom window and look down they'll regard as deadbeat an old car like this. Best you're not seen getting out of it in those shoes.'

'How do you think she'll laugh, Harpur?' Iles replied. 'Uproariously?'

'Uproariously,' the ACC said.

'That's one of the well-known ways people do laugh, sir. How about you?' Harpur asked.

'What?'

'Do you laugh uproariously as well? I visualize it. The two of you in your lovely home with a garage, double garage, laughing uproariously about it, very together. Or do you, personally, laugh in a different well-known style? She uproariously, but you drily? Hollowly?' A curtain moved in the bedroom of a neighbouring house. 'You shouldn't hang about, sir.'

'And what happened, Detective Chief Superintendent, after you had repaired the Sambrook boarding?'

'I drove the Assistant Chief Constable home.' The eyes and nose behind that curtain might turn up at the court, too.

'What time was that?'

'Just after midnight.'

'And did you simply decide then it would be a good moment for a visit to the Valencia district?'

'That's it.'

'Or did the Assistant Chief Constable order you to go there, as part of some operation involving the Sambrook house, together with the streets of the Valencia?'

They wanted to drag Iles in as well. 'I don't understand the question. Which operation?'
'Yes, which operation, Mr Denton?' the judge asked.

'There's a peeper, sir,' Harpur said outside Idylls.
'We're into break-up, Col.'
'Who? You and Sarah? Irretrievable breakdown through incompatible laughing?'
'The whole polity into break-up.'
'Polity? What's that?'
'Everything.'
'The old Chief used to worry about this,' Harpur replied.
'What?'
'Everything. Polity – if polity means everything. I think it must come with Staff rank.'
'What?'
'Worry. On such a grand, impressive scale. Don't slam the door. I'll pull it to quietly when you've gone, which should be now, sir.' Iles unfolded himself from the car. He glanced back once. He seemed about to give more thoughts on Sarah's special brand of laughter when remembering love with Harpur, but then turned and went through the open gate into his front garden. Harpur drove alone to the Valencia, parked and walked. It was a little before 1 a.m.
What would the ACC's chaos, or the inklings of chaos, look like if they were here? The changes – how would they show themselves? Harpur kept alert. He was recognized in the Valencia, naturally. Whenever he visited and walked, the word romped ahead of him by mobile, and the most obvious kind of street pushing paused. That had always happened, regardless of Iles's blind-eye regime. A kind of delicacy, a kind of tact and a kind of caution functioned – pushers pushed their product again as soon as Harpur had gone out of sight or left the area but, in the past, what dealers did not push while he could see them was their luck. Some token deference to Harpur's rank and dignity

53

was required. All right, pushers had been given the Iles nod, especially if they were from Ralph's or Manse's outfit, and as long as they stayed in designated spots, and didn't war. But they must not get flagrant. Also, dealers had known Iles's policy remained deeply unofficial and deeply fragile and could be abruptly overruled. They would wonder whether Harpur's presence meant it had been already overruled, and that he had been sent by someone above Iles to signal no more lawlessness. This was how they used to think, and they'd temporarily shut shop, tell clients to hang back.

Now, though, perhaps chaos – the gathering chaos, as foreseen by Iles – this chaos would mean complete indifference to Harpur. Who cared where he walked or when? Who gave a fuck any longer for his rank and dignity? Permissiveness had set in, and from the very top, so it was sure to last. These were easy streets, guaranteed, stable, governmentally blessed. In the new way of things, would trade go smoothly, uninterruptedly on – Harpur around or not – as the clubs turned out and their customers looked for something to carry them through the rest of the night and beyond? Of course, it had always gone on inside clubs like the Eton Boating Song and Nexus, regardless of Harpur on a pavement plod. Street dealing from cars or motorbikes or pedal bikes or on foot would be the true indicators tonight. And suddenly and sickeningly, Harpur realized that, if they all ignored him, he'd feel annihilated. Christ, was it because he'd really *enjoyed* getting them scared? Mr Power. Mr Pure. Mr Strut-by-Night. What would he add up to once he failed to make them scamper? Had their fright brought him his status and identity, the way other boxers' fright once brought Mike Tyson his? If this ability to scare disappeared would Harpur's own personal chaos start? Didn't he amount to anything without street-corner salaams?

But it was still there, thank God, their lovely, intelligent, respectful fear. Or *something* was there. As ever, they stopped the sly commerce when he appeared – *before* he appeared, having been buzzed a warning. They stood

54

around, or sat around in their cars, chatting, joshing, gorgeously inconsequential, as if taking a medicinal bit of air and comradeship at 1 a.m., and that was all. Harpur felt almost an affection for them, these crook custodians of his self-esteem. He saw people he knew. Of course, he saw people he knew. This was his little domain. He didn't hurry. He could savour their respect – D.W. Sangster-Thame, Bernard Moreton, Untimely Grace, Saul Evans, Phil Evans, Pompommed Frank. He paused a few times and gossiped with D.W. and Grace and Saul about the weather, the euro, television shows, the railways and National Health Service. Reciprocity filled the air between them and him on his route like really excellent music – say Stax Soul. Now, it seemed crazy to have thought this gorgeous, tame understanding between police and policed might collapse. Had he slipped into hysteria? Harpur was ashamed. When, months ahead, the defence lawyer in the Valencia shootings trial suggested Harpur had 'strolled' the area tonight, he would correct the word to 'walk', so as to make his visit sound purposeful, a duty, a routine patrol. But perhaps the lawyer had it right. Harpur felt so relieved now that, yes, he did relax and stroll, soothed by this fine, magnificently established response from the trade. Thank God for ritual.

He was fond of these old streets – the big, multi-flatted, unkempt but stately Victorian houses, iron-grilled shops and the huge, ugly Anglican church. A century or more ago this had been a prosperous area, the houses occupied by merchants and sea captains and their servants, the shops classy, the church influential. Harpur approved of history. It made him feel like the culmination of something – something he could pass on to his children so that in time *they* could become the culmination of something. Tomorrow he must tell Iles he should not be alarmist. This would really shake the ACC. Iles admired coolness and considered he had a lot of it, leaving aside paroxysms about his wife and Harpur.

He went on, doing Valencia Esplanade's whole length, and reached the Eton Boating Song, a handsome one-time

55

sailing vessel, moored in the marina now and skilfully adapted as floating restaurant and select drinking club. Some select drugs business went on there, too. Harpur knew, though, that if he went aboard no evidence of this would show. As soon as he put a foot on the gangplank, or even before, the alert would sound – what Harpur called 'inaction stations'. He did not need to test this. It was the same kind of satisfying normality encountered along the Esplanade. Things were all right. The *status* remained gloriously *quo*. His bit of cop grandeur stayed secure. He could go home eventually and still feel worthy of his daughters. Naturally, they would not have understood why he'd been uncertain of that, because they despised almost all police values, as most kids around their ages did. Just the same, it was important to Harpur.

He wanted to get back to them now. They would be in bed and asleep, he hoped, but he shouldn't leave them alone too long. Single-parenting was a real job, especially when Denise couldn't get to Arthur Street for the night. Jill had jumped in fast and unprompted with the assurance for Harpur that she believed Denise's excuse, which meant there was reason for *not* believing it. Occasionally, Jill did try to save him pain.

He decided he wouldn't walk back to his car along the Esplanade again but go through Stave Street. This was more direct and, in any case, it would look perverse and egomaniac to require all that kowtowing from pushers and suspension of trade a second time in one night. He'd done his checking and felt comforted. Anything extra would be oppressive, outside the terms of the Iles covenant.

At the murder trial later in the year, defence counsel wanted to know from Harpur how he came to be in Stave Street at exactly the right time to witness the killings that night. Behind them, the questions had a suggestion he had been tipped off an attack was scheduled – a suggestion also that he did nothing to stop it, either because he wanted the people concerned to wipe one another out, or because he wanted to watch and collect evidence

56

against the gunmen – 'evidence, Detective Chief Superintendent, for use in this very trial.' What the lawyer meant – meant without actually saying it – was that Harpur had connived at the deaths by letting them happen. Maybe he hadn't actually set up the situation, but he had used it. Dark opportunism.

'I'd already looked at one part of the Valencia district. Now, I wished to see other sections.'

'Could you tell us why, Detective Chief Superintendent?'

'Thoroughness.'

'Was it inspired thoroughness?'

'Police thoroughness.'

'Ah. Yes, police thoroughness. Was it thoroughness inspired by special knowledge?'

'Thoroughness. Elementary thoroughness.'

'Do you understand what I mean when I say special knowledge?'

'Special knowledge.'

'Detectives receive secret whispers from informants in the underworld, do they not, Detective Chief Superintendent – as a factor in police thoroughness?'

'Sometimes.'

'Do you receive such confidential matter from informants?'

'Sometimes.'

'Sometimes. I would like to ask whether this time – 1.40 in the morning – you might have been present in Stave Street to see this carnage because you had been told it would take place.'

Harpur could have replied, I'd satisfied myself up to this point that chaos had not set in and now I wanted to get home as quickly as possible to dad responsibilities, even though my girlfriend wasn't waiting there in bed but might be God knew where. 'No such information had come to me.'

One of the earliest lessons lawyers learned was, Do the damage in the question. You could smear someone just by asking, and probably reasking. The answers, the denials didn't matter all that much. The questions floated the possibility, and people would remember, regardless of the reply. That's what would happen to Harpur at the trial, when it came. The implication lingered that he had contacts in the drugs firms, might even have an involvement in a drugs firm and so could cleverly anticipate events, perhaps in his own interests, perhaps in the interests of some favoured outfit. Such questions could diminish a witness, make the rest of his evidence unreliable. The smear was more dangerous because, of course, Harpur certainly used informants from inside the drugs firms. He'd have been a dud operator if not. A detective was as good as his finks. On top of this, Harpur did have an involvement in the trade, if putting up with it on Iles's orders was involvement, or if open toleration under the new Chief's let-things-be policy was, or talking to D.W. Sangster-Thame and Untimely Grace about the euro and NHS.

He had walked about thirty metres down Stave Street when he saw D.W., Bernie Moreton and Pompommed Frank running towards him – really serious running. Harpur's daughters had made him watch a film called *Reservoir Dogs* on video, and these three moved at the all-out, terrified pace of a jewel robber chased by police early on in the picture. He didn't think the three were running from police, though. Like the villain in the film, Bernie had a handgun, something neat-looking, maybe a .44 Charter Bulldog, but carried in a way that made Harpur feel Moreton didn't really know how to use it. Why think this? Bernie held the revolver against his trouser leg and pointed down as he ran. Occasionally, he'd lower his head for a moment to glance at it, as though to remind himself the pistol was there and that he might even have to fire. It seemed strange to him, and the idea of shooting stranger. Bernie, like so many, had grown accustomed to peace.

Stave Street. It was wide, with big houses flatted as on the Esplanade, but here some had slipped so far into decay they stood abandoned or might have squatters. A few were boarded, like Curly's place on the Ernest Bevin. Not long ago Harpur placed an undercover girl in a flat here for anonymity, but since his familiarity with the street then, this bit of the locality definitely seemed to have sunk further. It appeared ready for demolition now, and for some extension of the marina development to be built on the site, dinky in cement brick. Two oval grassed islands lay line ahead in the centre and originally must have made the street mirror a smart London square. Possibly the council still gave the grass a rough cut now and then, and cleared most of the litter, although a ditched fridge stood there with its door hanging open on one hinge, and a conked-out computer. If there was shooting the fridge might give a little cover for anyone who went low. In their heydays these houses could still never have produced rubbish of this distinction. Sometimes Harpur didn't mind bulky dumped stuff. You had to think of what took over from it. Discards gave an uplifting message of renewal, progress, state of the art.

For a few minutes, Harpur and the three dealers were the only people in the street. They saw him and one of them – probably Pompommed – started shouting, but the distance was too great and his voice too weak, because most of what breath he had stoked his legs. Perhaps they'd recognized Harpur and it was a call for help. But help how, against what? Police did give help, didn't they? Harpur had no gun, of course, and if this turned into a shoot he wouldn't be able to do much more than radio call.

It turned into a shoot. Suddenly, there were more men in the street. Behind D.W., Bernie and Pompommed came another four, also running, all carrying handguns. Harpur thought he recognized two of them, perhaps three – layabout thugs, buyable by anyone with a stack, not strange to guns and not wrongfooted at the thought of using them. The fourth man, the one Harpur didn't know, had sprinted ahead of the other three and seemed in charge. They were not wrongfooted at all, and came very fast after Sangster-Thame, Bernie and Pompommed Frank. Harpur yelled at full, while taking out the handset: 'Halt. Armed police. Lay down your weapons. Armed police. Halt.' Perhaps it was heard. Perhaps it was heard and believed. Or maybe not. Nobody halted. Nobody dropped a weapon. Instead, the firing began. Bernard Moreton with his pistol looked as if

59

he might be making for the fridge and hoped to defend it like a bunker. He didn't get there, though.

'By remarkable chance, then, Detective Chief Superintendent, you began to walk along Stave Street and saw running towards you Donald Wade Sangster-Thame, Bernard Hugh Moreton and Frank Calhoun?'

'By chance, yes.'

'This was 1.40 a.m., so the street would be dark, wouldn't it?'

'The street was lit.'

'Do you know how many street lights were functioning in Stave Street that night?'

'Not exactly.'

'Not exactly. Would it surprise you to hear that, because of vandalism, only two out of eight lamps operated that night, according to the council Works Department?'

'The street was reasonably lit.'

'Reasonably. Only reasonably. Yet you have told the court you can say as a certainty who of these seven men in a dark street fired at whom and which of them was responsible for each of the four deaths. Is that credible?'

'I've said I wouldn't call the street dark.'

'I know you've said you wouldn't call the street dark. But is a street six hundred metres long and lit by only two lamps likely to look like noonday, Detective Chief Superintendent?'

'Nobody has claimed it looked like noonday.'

Afterwards, Harpur guessed the shooting lasted about four minutes. It seemed longer while it went on – a battle with distinct, separate, foully themed stages. Pompommed Frank carried big flab in the upper body and gut and soon grew exhausted. He fell back behind D.W. and Bernie, a long way back, and they left him, never slackened to help Pompommed keep up. He took a decision then, a feeble, fucking stupid decision. Watching him, Harpur could actually see it happen, this dopey process. The running was too much and he stopped, took a lean against some railings above a basement then pushed open the little gate there and as fast as he could went down the steps, clutching the handrail. Perhaps he thought he could dodge out and hide. He had his body hunched over, as though he believed this would make him less visible. Possibly he hoped people in the garden flat would let him in, give shelter.

God, could he have picked worse? Mind paralysis. Harpur, speaking into his radio, watched a lad he had identified as Sean Paderson detach himself at once from the hunting group, come to the railings around the steps, lean over and take a proper two-handed aim down, no hurry. He fired three shots, seconds between each, from what might be a 9 mm Browning automatic. It looked as if he wanted to be sure Pompommed had stopped moving, was finished, and so bang, then bang then . . . *oh, the fucker's still twitching* . . . bang. Harpur couldn't see Pompommed, but when the body was recovered later in the night from the bottom of the steps there were two head wounds and one in his wrist, the recovered bullets from a 9 mm Browning automatic.

The other three in the pack ran on. D.W., also obviously near exhaustion, turned and seemed to try and plead with them, actually arm-waving for emphasis, exposing his chest like a novice. He'd always had some oratory, D.W. Wasn't his father a clergyman? Malcolm Dean and a mate Harpur thought could be Jason Liddiard fired two shots each at him while still at a good trot, the guns probably .38 revolvers. D.W. fell to the pavement in mid-gesture. Harpur was sprinting towards them by now, still yelling he was armed and hoping to sound like a bristling posse. Chaos, chaos, chaos. Oh, yes, it had arrived, after all.

Bernie slanted away on to the environmental island, possibly making for the fridge. The three went after him. The fourth man, the chieftain, kept his stride but lifted his pistol, maybe another Browning automatic, and seemed to fire at the back of Bernie's head. He missed. Bernie kept going, though much slower now, not hurt, weak, tired. Then he suddenly stopped, still five or six metres from the fridge, spun around, as if realizing at last that he had a gun

61

and must use it. Perhaps he'd heard the bullet go past his head and guessed the next one probably wouldn't. He knew he would not make the cover and that even if he did, so what? He raised the weapon, single, stiff arm, and fired three times very rapid – so perhaps Bernie did know guns, after all.

The leader was stopped instantly. These were big, big rounds. It would only take one to smash him at this distance and maybe Bernie got him with more than that. His legs seemed to entwine with each other and his head dropped forward uncontrolled, as if something in his neck or backbone had been carried away. He tumbled down on Malcolm Dean's shoes. At once, he and Liddiard shot Bernie twice each.

They bent and picked up the leader and his piece and began to carry him back towards the top of the street, feet dragging, their arms crossed over his back and hands in his armpits. Paderson joined them from dealing with Pompommed and, as Harpur grew nearer, turned and fired a burst. But Dean and Liddiard might have lurched as they tried to get along fastish with their burden and knocked against Paderson. The barrage went askew and Harpur dived to crouch behind the fridge door. After half a minute he put his head around it and was about to start after them once more, but Paderson fired again and Harpur heard a bullet bang against the fridge body and into the ground near his foot. He shielded himself and when next he looked a big Peugeot had appeared at the top of the street and the three shoved the leader on to the rear seat, then got into it at a rush front and back and disappeared.

The armed response team arrived about three minutes later, took Harpur aboard their vehicle, and they searched for the Peugeot, around the Valencia first, then widening. Support cars joined in soon after but they all failed to find it. Instead, Dean, Liddiard and Paderson were picked up on Harpur's identification next day. A couple of tramps found the fourth man dead from gunshot wounds under a river bridge in the evening. His pockets had been cleared but fingerprints put a name to him – Clement Liss Vayling, more hirable heaviness, brought in from Liverpool. The burned-out stolen Peugeot turned up in a woodland spot famed for car pyres.

'Only one gun was recovered after the shooting, was it not, Detective Chief Superintendent?'

'Yes.'

'I believe this was a Charter Arms Bulldog revolver and had been used by Bernard Hugh Moreton.'

'Yes.'

'Experts have matched this pistol with the bullets that killed Vayling, have they not?'

'Yes.'

'No other gun has been found?'

'No.' There was the river. There were two docks still working. There might be accomplices who could see to the car and take the weapons right out of the scene.

'So, it is impossible for experts to match the bullets that killed Sangster-Thame, Moreton and Calhoun. Is that correct?'

'Yes.'

'And yet you still say Paderson killed Calhoun and that Dean and Liddiard killed Sangster-Thame and Moreton?'

'I saw them.'

'But you couldn't have seen Calhoun killed, could you? He was out of your sight at the bottom of the steps.'

'I saw Paderson fire down at him.'

'So you didn't actually see Calhoun hit?'

'I saw Paderson fire down at him with a 9 mm Browning pistol. The bullets found in the body or near it were from a 9 mm Browning.'

'Detective Chief Superintendent, it is the case of Sean Paderson, Jason Liddiard and Malcolm Dean that only Clement Liss Vayling of their party fired that night, and that they had accompanied him in an effort – tragically unsuccessful, as we know – had accompanied him solely to prevent his using a firearm, aware that he had a reputation for turning savage when he believed himself crossed.'

'I saw the deaths. Paderson, Liddiard and Dean all carried firearms.'

'Yet none of these weapons has been found?'

'Neither has Vayling's, and it's not disputed he had one.'

'You have told the court that you yourself had to take self-protective action. Nobody doubts that you behaved bravely. But could you really have maintained full observation in those circumstances?'

'I saw the deaths.'

No more of the missing weapons ever surfaced. Paderson, Liddiard and Dean would all be acquitted for lack of evidence, and because Harpur's sole testimony looked diseased – was brilliantly, legitimately and unscrupulously made to look diseased by the defence. Perhaps some residents in those Stave Street flats that night had their sleep broken by guns popping and came to the window. But, as Denton QC said, the light was imperfect. And, in any case, the Valencia area currently did not house many folk who'd risk aiding the police on a gang murder case. Because of that sparkling, much-reported cross-examination and the eventual not guilty verdicts, Harpur's reputation dissolved. He knew he was hurt through evil fluke – his accidental presence at the killings. In fact, of course, he also knew that fluke was neither evil nor good, just fluke, blood brother of true chaos and spotted when it was yet a great way off by the Assistant Chief.

Chapter Four

Ralph Ember had a message from Sashaying Vernon. Ember greatly approved of how it came. This was so different from the way Denzil just turned up at the Monty as if entitled. Someone *did* turn up at the Monty, but not Vernon himself, unannounced and presumptuous. One of his people came, hand delivering a letter in a properly sealed envelope, the stationery cream and thick, though not embossed or anything loud like that. Ember certainly did not object to a courier at the Monty. This rated as normal business procedure. He willingly gave the man a lager. What he detested was the cockiness of behaviour like Denzil's – the gross hint of equality and of a right to confront Ember even within the entirely personal walls of his club.

My Dear Ralph,
It was grand to see you the other evening at the Monty. I know my two lawyer friends, Rosie and Matthew, took with them back to London fine memories both of yourself and the club. Little had they expected to find such an admirable host and such a fine venue so far off the metropolitan map. This was, though, a rather informal and slightly hurried meeting and, in view of certain developments lately which I know I don't need to itemize here, a lengthier and more constructive 'get-together' might be à propos. Do you think I could give you dinner at the Grenoble, 8 p.m., Thursday? Or some other day and time, but soon.

Best,
Vernon

Maybe the fucker thought if you mentioned a restaurant with a French name you had to put in a bit of French, too, such as *à propos*. But that was all right. Sashaying liked to do style, and Ralph obviously regarded himself as in touch with any French element, because until lately he'd placed his daughter over there. *Grand* to see you. *Give you* dinner. These were big-timer, hearty words, like from a company chairman. Vernon would really have a go. No wonder they called him Sashaying. Ralph adored the *certain developments lately*. Oh, just a matter of Curly Sambrook and his daughter, then four people slaughtered down the Valencia, one a club member, as were two of the slaughterers, alleged. He found a Monty business card and wrote on the back, *Grenoble, 8 Thurs., fine, R.W.E.* He put this in a Monty envelope and gave it to the messenger for Vernon. The brevity and casualness Ralph considered suitable. Of course, he had monogrammed notepaper in a leather folder on the drawing-room rosewood table at home in Low Pastures, but this was hardly for messages to minor items like Sashaying. People of Ember's station didn't mess about with a lot of oozy wordage or decent grade stationery when they were in touch with a struggler, very luckily bailed from jail and liable to be back in there when his case came on again. Although Sashaying might have commercially relevant material to offer at a meeting, he could not be regarded as anything but jumped-up and fragile and must not expect more than formally polite treatment from a figure of Ralph's standing at this stage.

In normal times, he would not have allowed Vernon even that. If the rumour was right and he ordered the attack on Curly Sambrook's place, this would make him for ever intolerable to Ember. In some instances, Ralph might be able to understand extreme business competition, but not the disgustingly haphazard method used at Sambrook's place. There'd been terrible disregard for other lives in the house, including a child's. Of course, Ember did realize that during the present dark state of things any member of one's family might be a target. It was why he had brought Venetia home. But Lorraine Sambrook had *not* been a target. Curly was, and perhaps fair enough, but to get him they carelessly and inhumanly risked everyone else in the house. 'Collateral damage', in the shady language of soldiers. Did Sashaying suggest this, endorse it? Of course, another rumour said Curly had grassed someone and suffered for it, with his family.

And then there were the menaces charges still outstanding against Vern, and a possible connection with some of the people named in that disgraceful Valencia battle – more little-man commercial rivalry. If Ralph had felt able to follow his usual social and business rules, Sashaying Vernon could never have secured a one-to-one meeting with him, no matter how nicely the invitation was made and the excellence of the notepaper. Usually, Ember would avoid all closeness, knowing that to be associated with such a specimen brought vast risk, and that there could be no positive impact from this link upon his plan to lift the Monty to the level of the Athenaeum or Boodle's. As a joke some people referred to Ralph as 'Milord Monty'. He did not mind this. Despite the humour, it showed they saw where he was aiming. He liked the name, Boodle's, for an eminent club. It had a kind of silly childishness to it, as if the members didn't give a shit about what ordinary people thought – like the way some upper class people dressed, with old yellow and red weave sports jackets and so on. Once he got the Monty on a climb he might think about changing the name – not to Boodle's, obviously, as that was already in use, though something just as lovably stupid. Traddle's? Hobbidy's? Many a distinguished person loved playfulness. Didn't someone say the vital quality for a great soldier was gaiety?

But in the new trade situation, even his worries about the club and about increased danger for himself and the family had to be forgotten. No, not forgotten, or he would never have taken Venetia out of her Bordeaux school. No, not forgotten, but downplayed. There were enormous uncertainties. Nothing was predictable. Denzil hinted he might try to displace Mansel Shale. Would it get further than talk? Was Denzil capable of that kind of smart violence? How would things develop if he did manage the takeover? How would they develop if he tried and botched it? What effect would the new liberalizing have on prices and returns? Would Iles ever get back his dominance and ability to run a sensible, healthy drugs policy based on careful and selected permissiveness, but not this sickeningly general, flagrant licence?

Ralph didn't have answers and in his confusion was ready to look at all proposals from anyone who amounted to something, and Vernon just about did. After all, he had built up a sound income, kept alive and undisabled, and knew how to pick lawyers. That pair were truly gifted – able to get Vern bail despite everything and recognize the qualities of Ralph and the Monty. He might confer on some kindly folk free membership of the club for a year when it assumed its new personality. Sashaying had one other advantage. He was not Denzil and therefore probably safer as to Venetia, especially if Sashaying had to run any possible partnership with Ralph from in jail with a fine sentence, regardless of Rosie and Matthew. Menaces was serious.

Ember could see a various day ahead. This evening he would need to get down to the Valencia and do an individual assessment of what damage that outrageous incident the other night had caused to his people and to business generally there. Such a survey was not something for a subordinate. He thought of a head of state in, say, some earthquake country deciding to visit the disaster site himself. The Valencia survey required Ralph's own quick eye, his own flair for appraisal. It was a question of measuring morale and mood. Traders who'd been used to a long period of peace were bound to feel upset when outright killings like that took place so near. But for Ralph to traipse Valencia streets would mean another break from his usual work pattern. He detested going to this district. Direct involvement there should not be necessary for him any longer. Surely he had moved above that. The grubbiness of the area and decay of the buildings sickened him.

He did not want to share a pavement with the sort of small-time low life that roamed the Valencia. But now, these killings and the overall change made his previous distancing of himself no longer wise. He had to know the new scene first hand. All sorts of mysteries clung to that gun battle, and not only to do with the future.

For instance, the word was Harpur had been in Stave Street at just the moment it all started, more than fifteen minutes before the main cop battalions arrived. And earlier he had done one of his baronial bloody swagger patrols along the Esplanade. What *was* this? How could there be such timing? Who'd been briefing him, and why? It was damned off-colour that a senior police officer should know more than Ralph, surely to God, and damned disturbing. All right, the whole scene had begun to unravel, but some basic trust should still be possible between established business stalwarts such as himself and senior law folk. 'A blessed rage for order.' This was a phrase he remembered from literature lectures in his Foundation Year on the mature student degree course down the road at the local university. He had suspended the course now, but parts of it stuck. These words came from an American poet, Wallace Stevens, and Ralph felt he had that blessed rage, too. Now, though, it did not work. Had Ralph been cut out? Who was Harpur in with – Manse? Sashaying? Someone even newer than Sashaying but heavy with sweetener funds? One of Ember's panics nibbled at him. He resisted – thank God, still *could* resist. *I'm Ralph W. Ember. Ralph W. Ember. Ralph W. Ember.* Often he'd repel panic with such resounding, utterly true inner reminders, repeated for as long as was needed.

These days, he had a 9 mm Beretta automatic in an upstairs boxroom at home in Low Pastures and he decided to give it a little check over this morning when he felt better and no longer needed to tell himself his name. His legs would definitely get him up the stairs even now, immediately, if he'd wanted to try them. Always Ralph had hated the need to keep a gun in a fine country property like Low Pastures. It seemed crude, a gross relic of more difficult days. The house had grounds, a paddock, stables, a library, exposed stone walls in authentic mode, and surely symbolized a different, dignified life for Ralph now. But the Beretta was there all the same among plenty of old invoices and receipts in a locked steel filing cabinet and occasionally he did still have to bring it out.

He would take it tonight to the Valencia. That was elementary trade practice in the new ambience. He hadn't needed actually to fire a weapon at anybody for really a longish while and, obviously, he'd got rid of that one immediately, and all surplus ammunition, then replaced it with the Beretta. Under the floorboards in the master bedroom he had a top of the range safe but that was sure to be one of the first places on any police search list if they ever grew evil, and it would be mad to keep a weapon and cartridges there. The filing cabinet was probably only a fraction better, but the gun lay under a lot of papers, and he could not leave it in some less secure part of the house because of Margaret and his daughters about the place. This was a home, for fuck's sake, no armoury.

The other assignment he had lined up for himself today was a visit with Margaret and Venetia to Corton House school to see whether the head could take Venetia. His younger daughter Fay was there and happy. Venetia had attended Corton before Ember transferred her to Poitiers, then Bordeaux, and Ralph greatly hoped she could have her place back. Despite dropping Latin and Greek and ignoring Ralph's protests, Corton remained one of the best private schools locally. The nice layout of the place, with a delightful little shaded quadrangle and pretty fountain, as well as a pair of lovingly tended pergolas in the gardens, meant it was easy to have a heavy or two around there pretty often keeping an eye, ready to really blast the fucking ventricles out of any louts who came to net Fay and now possibly Venetia also. Of course, you had to be careful picking the lads sent on a job that was basically ogling a girls' school for hours, where pupils wore damned attractive uniforms. But Ember talked with everyone given that duty and underlined there must be absolutely no approaches. He knew how to get his meaning through to staff, and it didn't require fancy writing paper.

He climbed the stairs, his legs terrific. These legs would be a plus on anyone. That panic had never got a proper grip. He felt triumphant, like someone who beat a disease by will alone. He went to the boxroom, closed the door to guard against interruptions and brought out the Beretta and a carton of bullets. It was a beautiful silver weapon and lovely to hold. Although in one way he loathed this gun for the slur it put upon everything that had been achieved in the commercial environment these last few years, he could also thrill to it. An automatic in his hand was bound to activate high-class memories of his own survival and the very necessary destruction of enemies. He loaded the full fifteen rounds in case of complications, then dug further into the filing cabinet drawer and brought out a shoulder holster. He took off his jacket, fixed the holster and buttoned down the Beretta in the pouch. He put his jacket back on and did it up.

The boxroom lacked a looking glass for Ralph to make sure he had no bulge under the left lapel, but he smoothed down the cloth a few times and thought it fine. He had on one of his Cachape and Drew made-to-measure pinstripe suits for the session at Corton. Quality at this kind of meeting signified. Obviously, the jacket was not tailored to conceal a 9 mm Beretta and holster harness, but the cut had generosity, and he would relax his body, keep his chest a bit concave. In any case, most likely the head at Corton was unaccustomed to eyeing up the suits of parents to see if they had a piece aboard.

But Margaret would be sharper. He did not want her made anxious – or more anxious. Obviously, she was already worried because Ralph had thought it best to bring Venetia home. She wouldn't take the bullshit about their daughter's French education now having reached completion. Margaret could see and feel the general changes in the commercial situation, and if she noticed Ralph had suddenly started to go armed it might really trouble her. Occasionally, she used to insist he should leave the trade and become wholly legit. Once, she took the children and left him because he wouldn't.* But, of course, she came back after not very long. He never punished her in the least for any of that. Margaret certainly had many good factors, and he constantly tried to think of them. In Ralph's view, this was what marriage meant. Ember might have postponed wearing the gun until he visited the Valencia late tonight, but he felt positive now, at this instant, glowing with non-panic, and thought the Beretta and the comforting pressure of the leather around his chest would help him keep this happy poise. Although he still craved the tranquillity that had prevailed for years, if it was no longer assured he must respond sensibly. He had always prized his ability to adapt. He was Ralph W. Ember, Ralph W. Ember, but now Ralph W. Ember with a Parabellum Beretta handy.

In the car on the way to Corton, Venetia said: 'God, dad, that carry-on down the Valencia, though. On TV News. I mean the *big* News, not just local. Wow, dad.'

It bothered Ralph that she spoke only to him about this – 'dad' twice – although Margaret was with them. Why should Venetia think he'd be so interested? No time since she came back from Bordeaux yet she had the feel of things. He'd always known she was a bright kid and full of instincts. Or had she picked up signs from that fucking know-all, Denzil? Was she seeing him? Signs might not be everything she'd pick up. 'Which carry-on, love?' he replied.

'People shot all over the place. Stave Street and wherever.'

'What do you know about Stave Street?' Ralph replied.

'On TV News, I told you.'

'All right. But I hope you don't go into the Valencia yourself,' he said. 'It's unnecessary.'

'What does that mean, dad – "unnecessary"?'

'This is an area where you'd never need to be, as I see things.'

* *Naked at the Window*

72

'Like a battlefield,' Venetia replied.

'The media exaggerate, you know.'

'There's four people dead. They gave names. How can they exaggerate?'

'The Valencia is its own world,' Ember said. 'What goes on there is confined to that area, those streets. It's of no consequence, except to the Valencia. That's always been the case.'

'Like a ghetto?'

'Of no consequence to the rest of the city. These people deal with their own little enmities, often in a disgustingly lawless but, happily, sealed-off way.'

'Little? Four knocked over.'

'Little in the sense of their significance in the wider, normal considerations of the city,' Ember replied. 'Look, I think we should keep our minds on the immediate problem, don't you – making sure we can get you on to Corton's register again?' He grinned in a very relaxed and fatherly style for a spell. 'I don't suppose we'll be discussing incidents at the Valencia when speaking to the head, nor referring to people "knocked over".'

It would not amuse Ralph to be walking around a select girls' school secretly tooled up – none of that hopelessly childish 'If they did but know' shit. The gun was a feature of the times, and an unfortunate feature, no more than that, the way people carried gas masks in World War II, or had to disinfect boots at farms during foot and mouth. Its significance in Ralph's life must be minimal. True, moments came when he'd have loved to shoot with at least eight rounds the smarmy cow running that Bordeaux school, but this was obviously only fantasy, and he definitely did not intend the Corton head to spot the gun and let Venetia back through mere fright. Ember knew there might be difficulties, if the head realized why he had moved Venetia abroad. A girl like Venetia, with her desires and blunt talk and so on, could bring a school problems. Ember would treat the interview carefully, diplomatically – definitely no more raging about the abandonment of Latin and Greek in favour of what he used to call 'soundbite Aeschylus'.

In the car they were all quiet for a while. Then Margaret said: 'You talk as if the Valencia's a different world, Ralph. Like Mars.'

'Exactly,' Ember replied. 'That's what it is.'

'Venetia's bound to hear about such things. She's almost grown up. We can't censor what she sees and reads,' Margaret said.

She was like this sometimes, but Ralph stayed entirely calm as to actual behaviour or words. Women often had insights, he would never deny that. Mostly, they should be given a fair ration of respect. Frequently, he really listened to Margaret. A wife had definite rights to be heard. But, oh, God, was it so clever after all to bring Venetia home from Bordeaux if she began rubbish topics like this and got Margaret on her side? He loved them and knew they loved him and wanted only good for him, but how could they understand matters? He had enough crises to bang into shape without these two and a fucking seminar on censorship. 'Of course Venetia must be aware of what goes on, darling,' he replied. 'It's just a question of focus.'

He had an idea Venetia, with her cleverness and her possible damn whispers from Denzil, thought he would probably know one or more of those deads through the Monty, and that was why she started on the Valencia. Did that slob Denzil put her up to it? She had never thought much of the Monty and used to call it 'a pit' sometimes, and 'the clink waiting room'. This was before France. Yes, even when quite young she had a mouth on her. Venetia said: 'I wondered if . . .'

'What, darling?' Ember replied.

'Well, were any of the deads –'

'I don't like that way of talking.'

Venetia was in the back and had been leaning forward between the two front seats to talk to Ember. Now, she folded herself away into the offside rear corner. 'Forget it,' she said. 'It doesn't matter.'

'What?' Ember asked.

'No, forget it, dad.'

'Stress your wish to get to Oxford or Cambridge eventually. That sort of ex-pupil is good for a school like Corton,' Ember replied. 'Balliol College, or Trinity. Don't just say university, because this could mean any of these new dumps around the country. The headmistress puts "Cantab." after her degree. "Cantab." is how they say Cambridge, like a code for the educated. People don't advertise "MA Crewe". Or maybe you could say you're aiming for the Sorbonne because of French, but that you'd never get into riots flinging cobblestones. That damn Revolution – they think disorder's a duty.' He'd made sure she wore a good dark skirt and decent blouse and jacket for this meeting.

Many had misunderstandings about the club, not just Venetia. All right, D.W. Sangster-Thame was a Monty member, of course, and Malcolm Dean and Jason Liddiard. But when they asked to join, Ember had no proper reason to exclude them. Acceptance would be much more difficult as the Monty began its transformation. These were exactly the kind of people Ralph *would* keep out, once the club moved towards Athenaeum or Boodle's level. Surely, never would you get members of either of these select London haunts in turf shoot-outs and smart-arse disposal of the weapons. Even with the Monty in its present status, Ralph hoped on decorum grounds he could discourage any post-funeral party in the club for D.W. Obviously, he sympathized with murdered folk and their relatives, villains or not, but quite often aftermaths produced difficult evenings at the Monty. Ember loathed having to punch women. The civilities of life were what he sought.

'Of course, in some ways it's good that Venetia is aware of districts like the Valencia and their dangers,' Margaret said. 'Young people are drawn to such areas – for kicks, as they call it. She'll be alert.'

'Slumming,' Ember replied. 'I think she'd be better off not going there at all.'

'Well, I'm sure you do, Ralph. But youngsters won't accept barriers to their activities, will they?'

'Dad, I don't think it's right there should be division marks across a city – some places all right, some bad. I mean, in Bordeaux –'

Oh, but hasn't she seen the fucking world? Who paid? 'Countries can certainly learn from one another,' Ember said. 'It would be narrow to dispute that.'

'People might be down the Valencia one day and anywhere else in the city on the next,' Venetia said. 'Think about the club, dad.'

'What about it?' He'd been completely right. Venetia had a scheme for this chatter. It might be her own, or she might have had help.

'Well, I mean, some of the people in that massacre down the Valencia could easily be members of the Monty, couldn't they? I'm not saying they are, but . . . well . . . a big, popular club like the Monty . . . it will have all sorts, won't it?'

'All sorts of what?' Ember asked.

'Types,' Venetia said.

'I try not to think of people as types, but as individuals,' Ember replied.

'You know what I mean, dad,' Venetia said.

'I don't see what you wish to prove, Venetia,' Ember replied.

'Like mum says, I've got to be able to look after myself,' she told him.

'We'll make sure you're looked after,' Ember said.

'Oh, dad!'

'Not possible continuously, is it, Ralph?' Margaret said. 'Not desirable.'

'Like, if you're . . . well . . . sort of *connected* to a scrape like that at the Valencia . . . that's through the club, I mean . . . the people, or some of them, in the Monty, in contact with you . . . well, the peril could reach you, couldn't it, dad, and maybe reach me? You're well known. I'm thinking of what Denzil said.'

And so here was the name. 'When?' he asked.

'You remember – when we were talking, the three of us.'

And later, just the two? Ember did not ask it, though.

'What did Denzil say?' Margaret asked.

'Nothing so very clear, but hints,' Venetia replied.

'About danger?' Margaret said.

'Peril! What a word,' Ember said. 'Like an old-fashioned adventure story.'

'What danger?' Margaret asked.

'Denzil is a dogsbody, with a dogsbody's mind and information,' Ember replied. 'Best you stay very clear of him if he's going to give you anxieties like that, Venetia.'

'*Were* some of them club people, dad?'

'Who says?' Ember replied.

'Just wondering.'

'Why?'

'The tie-up. Like I said,' Venetia replied. 'If I need to know.'

'I'm not familiar with every member of the club, Venetia.'

'No, but a list,' she replied.

'I've explained, love, that what happens in the Valencia is the Valencia's own concern, and only the Valencia's.'

'I've got to have street savvy,' Venetia said. 'To be savvy I need wising up. Wising up means I have to know connections.'

'Please don't spout Americanisms when we're with the head,' Ember said.

Venetia seemed to feel suddenly that the talk had become a bit argumentative and she sat forward again in more friendly style and, as if to reassure Ember about the Corton meeting, touched him lightly, passing her hand affectionately from the left shoulder of his jacket down over the lapel. He knew she must have felt the loaded holster, but she did or said nothing to indicate that. Her hand made no pause from shock or curiosity even for a moment. 'We'll be fine, dad,' she told him. 'I'll behave like an intelligent mouse. One thing they teach you in France is how to put up a good show – how to make the most of yourself.'

'Thanks, Venetia,' Ember replied. *How to make the most of yourself.* But *he* was not sure what to make of her. Did she expect him to wear armament and therefore took the

Beretta as normal and not worth asking about? Or was she surprised by the gun but wise enough and considerate enough to keep quiet about it so as not to disturb Margaret? This kid had acuteness.

They parked in the school yard and walked through the quadrangle towards the head's study. Ember remembered the geography quite well, but looked about carefully, reminding himself of detail. When he reasoned that protection of the two girls would be fairly easy here, he didn't mean the guardians could hang about unseen in the grounds. No, they'd really look deeply apish in this refined setting. So would any thugs who came hunting for Fay and Venetia, though – nice and obvious. Most of the quadrangle and gardens were visible from a couple of streets outside and he'd tell his people to drift about there, in cars, on foot, with plenty of personnel changes, so they wouldn't look like stalkers. God, but what an imperative, the welfare of his kids! This was where Man had such wonderful affinities with animals and Nature generally – preservation of offspring to secure the future. He would have liked to put his hand on the Beretta now and cosset the trigger but that could not be done unnoticed because it would require unbuttoning the holster flap and lifting the gun out – improper for this location unless, of course, actual thugs did show.

'My – or I should say *our* – concept of a true education is to do with width, range, not some dismally narrow focus on what might be "useful" in later life,' Ember remarked to the headmistress. 'This, we feel, is admirably provided by Corton. The spell of schooling in France was, naturally, also intended to help with this width and range. I'm a great believer in what used to be called, I think, "the whole man" – or woman, definitely – that is, the pupil whose total personality is enlarged and enhanced by gifted teaching, and more than teaching, the, as it were, prevailing *ethos* and *values* of the establishment.'

Did he have to spend all his fucking life talking to schoolies? He never felt sure with this one whether she saw his resemblance to the young Charlton Heston, which was often remarked on by women, and which could bring favours of all sorts. He turned his head a little so she could get some of his fine cragginess now. To refuse to take a girl back into the classroom was not something many would have the gall to do to El Cid, even a girl with awkward urges, like Venetia.

'Which is why Margaret and I are always positive about contributions to school projects – the theatre, the swimming pool – since these are part of that larger notion of education we espouse,' Ember said. 'With Corton we can feel part of a developing *process*, not merely of an institution that is fixed and unadventurous.'

He wanted to keep talking so that Venetia did not get an opening to say much. You could never be certain what she would come out with. She used conversation to cut through to things and was not old enough yet to realize that some things should *not* be cut through to. For instance, any over-accurate account of why she had left Corton House and now needed to come back might fuck up the whole scheme. All right, although Venetia could detect a Beretta and not yell out, there were other aspects of tact where she would be less strong. Ember did not want his wife to intervene unduly either. Margaret was certainly sensible, but, like Venetia, lacked flair in the buttery way of speaking which would help now.

'Theatre, for instance,' Ralph said. 'Who could deny participation in quality drama brings unmatchable revelations as to the human state? Oh, yes, these works can be read in the study, but to enact them on stage – this is surely another matter, a greater, more memorable experience. Think of that *Mousetrap* going on for years, decades, in London. Then *Waiting for Godot* or *Les Mis*. These are insights. Would *The Mousetrap* have lasted if it didn't offer such insights on humankind to generation after generation, yet in entertaining form? Some use the term "thesp" as mockery. Myself, I have to demur at that.'

Joy. It amazed him, but this had to be the word. He was

down at the Valencia in the night, expecting to find fear and torn morale among traders, but no, he encountered . . . Yes, yes, yes, joy. At first, the streets had seemed simply normal – commerce proceeding as usual. This surprised him enough. But then, when he talked to folk, he heard only soaring notes of confidence and optimism. Everyone was so fucking brilliantly, gloriously *positive*. For a little while he wondered, was he misreading things? After all, he brought with him his own feelings of relief now Venetia had been fully fixed up at Corton that morning – start Monday, one year's fees in advance, as with Fay, and the usual unspoken commitment to chip in for improvements to the swimming pool, astronomy gear and the theatre's acoustic system, now at double rate because of two girls. Perhaps this happiness at the school success made him imagine happiness in others, like, *Laugh and the world laughs with you*. Not so. Not a bit. The good spirits were out there, all around him, matching his own, perhaps, but separate, real. Ember hated this area, still hated it, but tonight it could thrill him. He let it thrill him.

'Ralph! Here's my mother,' Bart Haverson said. He'd been dealing in the Valencia for at least eighteen months, always taking his supply from Ember, always up to the mark with payments, a real piece of loyalty. Bart had a fine location in and around an all-night caff next to the one-time Zoar Noncon church, now the Parasol club. 'Lovely of you to visit. This is Ralph, ma, like I talked to you of him often. He sees to me wholesale. Only the best.' Bart would be around forty, his long black leather coat of terrific quality, a credit to him and the herd it came from. Ralph saw an increased number of great leather garments around lately and wondered if some sharp bugger had been digging up foot-and-mouth corpses and skinning wholesale.

'Of course I heard of you, Mr Ember – all the commodities, and then your club as well, a good welcome there for many,' Mrs Haverson replied, 'and so much more class than the Parasol, I'm sure. Oh, I'll say.'

'The Monty has its own, possibly different, style, yes,' Ember replied.

'Ma's thinking of doing some pushing personally, Ralph – I mean, in the new, favourable conditions of trade OKness. The older person market. She sees a gap. A lot of disposable income even now with the pensions cut-backs. People of that age, they need good trips so they can forget their prostate and teeth problems, and not just trips with Saga. I know she'd be happy to take from you, same as myself.' Mrs Haverson wore black leather, also, but a skirt and jacket suit. Her trainers were top range.

'Lord, that wonderful operation, Mr Ember,' she said.

'Which?'

'Harpur,' she replied.

'Did you put him up to it, Ralph?' Bart asked.

'What?'

'Oh, I understand. You got to play opaque, obviously,' Bart said. 'Confidentiality.'

'This will be the making of the Valencia,' Mrs Haverson said. 'Everyone knows that. You can *feel* it.'

And, yes, Ember could. 'Put him up to what, Bart?' he asked.

'Oh, it's all right, Ralph. Safe to talk. Ma's really discreet.'

'When Bart says "older person market", we don't mean eventide homes, Mr Ember. They wouldn't let me in to sell, and a lot of those nests control their inmates' money, so they wouldn't be able to buy much, anyway. No, I'm thinking of restaurants with a special rate for elderlies if they eat before 7 p.m. Or trad jazz evenings in pubs where the crowd is going to be antique, like the music. *My* kind of jazz. Nothing later than the Hot Five, 1929. Well, Bart said to me as soon as we heard, he said, "That'll be Ralph."'

'How do you mean?' Ember replied.

'Put out the whisper to Harpur so he's there spot on time – Stave Street,' Mrs Haverson said. 'And leads to seven of them taken out. Four dead, three inside. These were seven warring idiots, Mr Ember. As you know, obviously. And knew. A nuisance to the district, and making things dangerous for everyone, tainting the new regime. Just mad freelances, no system to them, no respect for anyone's turf. Damn guns everywhere. But not now – because of your sweet scenario with Harpur. Bart said you'd be exactly the one to get it in advance there was going to be gunplay and to see the grand possibilities. You'd have the flair, and you talk to Harpur sometimes, don't you, a rapport? I was born in Stave Street, you know. I've never seen the Valencia so serene, not in sixty-two years, Mr Ember. You deserve a lot of credit. Your domain. And, because it's yours, it's ours, too. We can all take pride in it. I see you're tooled up under that great piece of cloth, but not necessary now, beautifully not necessary.' She moved forward suddenly and gave Ember a long kiss on the lips. 'I expect people have told you you look like Charlton Heston the way Charlton Heston *used* to look.'

'Charlton Heston?' Ralph replied with one of his fine chuckles. 'You mean the film star? *Ben Hur*? That's a new idea, I must say, Mrs Haverson.'

'Delphine,' she said. 'Or simply D.'

Some men these days didn't mind older women too much. Himself, Ralph could not quite get the taste. He thought he might work on it, but when he was older.

Chapter Five

Constructive – this was how Mansel Shale saw himself. That above all. So he felt sad Denzil most probably had to be removed. This was bound to be an upset for the firm. On the face of it, anyway, Denzil was only Mansel's driver. Just the same, it would be an upset nearly as big as when Alfie Ivis got shot to death in his own property.* Alf could be a raging thicko, yes, but he did have a flair or two and at the time of that incident rated as more or less Manse's first mate. Definitely Shale did not see to his slaughter, either direct or through orders. With Denz things might have to be different, and this turned Manse sad because no way could you regard killing a staff member as constructive.

Denzil looked like he escaped from one of them old jail ship hulks in drama on TV, but he had been with Manse a fair while. Always Shale tried to treat him totally decent, hoping he might climb to be a proper human one day in the current era. True, now and then Denz's verbiage had to be beat right back or the fucker would push you into coma with his ideas, or what you might *call* ideas, for kindness. But Shale hardly ever closed the partition screen in his Jaguar to block off Denzil when he chauffeured. To do that often would of seemed rude and vain to Manse, no matter what a noisy twerp Denz was. Even driving he could talk back over his shoulder. Of course, this vain sod chipped about wearing the chauffeur's cap Manse bought for him because it told people he was what he was, a flunkey.

* *Pay Days*

Manse disliked the arguments over this. But he realized that people wanted to push themselves and become jumped-up, even a piece of ugly rubbish like Denzil.

Manse was jumped-up himself and knew it. To try to show he might not be, he lived in the old St James's ex-rectory and had a drawing room with Pre-Raphaelite paintings by Arthur Hughes and Edward Prentis. However, Shale saw that anyone who needed to *prove* they were not jumped-up had to do it because they were, like a drunk trying everything to walk straight. Think of poor Ralph Ember, hoping to magic that shit-hole of a club, the Monty, into a chic social spot.

Until now there had not been a thing about Denz to make Manse decide he better have him killed – not out-and-out *killed*. The way Manse regarded matters was, Denz could be managed and would often produce something quite useful for the firm, obviously on the crude, basic side. It was this kind of attitude to him, never mind all his faults, that Manse meant by constructive. But Manse knew what he in his personal self had a true richness of was instincts, and these started telling him lately there seemed something up with Denz. For now, Manse could not work out what. His instincts usually operated in a general way at first, which, as he viewed things, would probably be what *made* them instincts. If you actually learned some-thing as a total fact, you definitely did not need instincts because you'd be sure. He felt that the need in Denzil to jump up had started to get real strong. This baggage man would like to jump up as high as Manse himself and shove Manse out of the way to make room. Manse could feel treachery about.

Of course, in any sort of truly worthwhile commercial organization, them with boardroom positions, such as Manse, always feared treachery from below. He even used to wonder about Alfie Ivis. A chairman had to keep look-ing to make certain no sod was sawing the legs off of the chair. This was referred to as 'the rising generation' which could be seen in Nature as when the old stag is antlered by one of the young ones to fuck all the does himself. In

America, a famous school of business Manse had read about known as Harvard most probably gave a degree in get-ahead brutality. And it was not just commerce. Think how they finished Margaret Thatcher. When she cried in the car on the News after losing Number 10 Downing Street, them tears was about treachery, just that. Although there had always been stinking cheek and big envy in Denzil, which could be dealt with, Shale thought he spotted more than these now. He spotted a brain at work. All right, it was only Denz's sheep brain, but he might have help. Treachery.

The two firms, Shale's and Ralph Ember's, worked in a kind of very useful partnership. About every quarter, they held a joint company meeting and dinner at the Agincourt Hotel. Manse did not mind this place too much. It did medieval banquets most of the time with minstrels and so-called mead and waitresses wearing old-time gear to show tit. These days they was not allowed to cook swan for the punters as in the ancient feasts but did goose. Mondays the Agincourt stayed shut and the firms could hire its big dining room. This was a good arrangement. Manse and Ralph did not want all the medieval shit but there was a fine feel of space and comfort and they could name their own menu.

A meeting had been fixed for tonight, and although Manse never spent a poncy long time deciding which suit and tie, he aimed to pick a worthwhile combination, but subdued. He wanted to stay backgrounded as much as possible – low-profiled – so he could watch that laddie, Denzil, and see if he had something going with Ember, such as conspiracy. This must be a possible. Manse had to make the main trade position speech, and therefore would not remain absolutely unnoticed, but for the rest of the time he hoped he could just do some quiet observing. A little while ago, he bought a three-piece dark suit in the Oxfam shop for its genuine 1930s cut and grand, enduring cloth. Although Manse knew he might never get taken for an Old Etonian he thought he ought to try and believed this suit with its quality helped. It was obviously class, yet not bombastic, the lapels just like lapels should be. Shale thought lapels always spoke a message. This suit had come through the Second World War and helped show why we won. Hitler and Goebbels would never of had a suit like this – they capered around in uniforms and epaulettes and brass buckles all the time, but a suit of such style was unbeatable, like the British Navy. Manse put the suit on now and a grey tie with certain small designs on it which suited the historical aspect of the Agincourt's name – shields, lances, castle towers with loopholes – no in-your-fucking-face stripes.

There was another reason Manse planned to stay unflashy. It had seemed to him that, because of trade changes, a kindly thought would be to invite the two officers, Harpur and Iles. This Shale saw as an added constructive element, and to be constructive should surely be the chief aim of all commercial leaders. Ralph Ember had agreed to the approach after a bit of doubt-raising and nerviness – what you would expect from some jibberer often known as Panicking Ralph.

Of course, the thing about the Agincourt meeting was it could never be more than a show session – only for the sake of the work force. Harpur and Iles wouldn't learn a fucking thing about the firms, but it would be a plus for friendly relations and what was known as 'image' if the pair came. The real financial and other sensitive matters were, naturally, considered in private by Shale and Ember alone. Way back they both saw it would unsettle personnel if, for instance, they discovered Manse and Ralph drew £600,000 each a year from the firms – although staff's pay was tidy enough when you thought of, say, an assistant's in Marks and Spencer. Denzil could corner £50K despite his looks and voice. Manse and Ralph had decided then it would be damn stupid and even callous to get unrest going in the street pushers and so on by too much openness. On quite a few business procedures, Shale and Ember shared good agreement, though of course this did not mean Manse trusted that dodgy prince. What Manse realized was, very unpredictable times had suddenly shown up – the slackening of the law, the burning of Sambrook and his kid, the Valencia shootings. Hellish new pressures lined up. How Shale saw it was, Ralphy Ember had always adored the predictable, really *needed* it, and he might join with some bugger in unpredictable ways if he thought this might bring the lovely predictable back to him.

Shale had some weaponry in a wall-safe behind one of the Arthur Hughes pictures. He loved Pre-Raphaelite painting – all the terrific colours, especially vivid blue, and so many women with plenty of ginger hair, often right down their backs to the arse. Usually these models wore long dresses you could not see through, but flimsy and with a shine to them, their eyes glinting from thoughts about King Arthur or fucking the artist when the day's work finished. This was a time when anyone with an easel knew they had to give the customers some brightness, and not just brightness in sick little squares and dots like what was known as modern art but about *people*, with the kind of skin anyone would notice and long to provide a nice frame for. Clearly, Manse never let Denzil have the combination to that safe. Of course, though, he might have a gun of his own hidden somewhere, and Ralph Ember would definitely have one on him tonight, and obviously had one on him when he killed Ivis in his lighthouse property, though never no charges and never no trace of that gun, a .38 Smith and Wesson Bodyguard revolver, the Press said, based on Forensic's look at the bullet.

Denz lived in a flat at the top of the rectory. Naturally, he was a complete cunt about art and most probably never even heard of the Pre-Raphaelite Brotherhood and all their terrific aims. He'd think Raphaelite was plastic for making cheapo caff tablecloths. But Denz had most likely found the safe during little saunters around the house when Manse was away, and Shale changed the combination every couple of months, and always counted the guns and ammunition at least once a week. There were some very powerful pistols locked up and Manse would hate any of them to be adopted by a prick like Denz. It angered Shale to think of him lifting that picture off the wall to have a look at the safe. Paintings were items that should never get handled by Denzil even when under glass. He was wrong for beauty. Manse would not have thought this about Alfie Ivis. Sometimes, Shale felt it was out of order for Ember to have killed Ivis, though Alfie could be devious and unhelpful. Manse took a Heckler and Koch 9 mm automatic and filled the nine-round magazine. He put the gun into the pocket of his jacket, resecured the safe and hung the Arthur Hughes back on its hook. The police used this kind of pistol, and Shale thought them sensible.

He and Ember took it in turns to pay for the Agincourt occasion and it was on Manse tonight. Whoever paid also ran the meeting. Rising after the great goose dinner, he said: 'First and most obvious I got to declare how truly wonderful it is to see happily with us now Assistant Chief Constable Desmond Iles (Operations) and Detective Chief Superintendent Colin Harpur, boss of CID.' He led a bit of applause. Iles stood and gave a sort of small, stiff bow like a lesson in the way to head-butt. Harpur just sat there staring around, that snoop way of his, but anyone could see he was real worried about his daughter and Iles, which all had heard the rumours of.

Manse said: 'Undoubted, some outside and even some with us now, might consider it strange to find two important police officers at what is a companies business meeting. But, myself, I regard it totally natural they should be here as a pleasant sign of certain recent changes in what could be referred to as "the commercial climate", and I know my colleague, Ralph, shares this opinion.'

'Indeed, yes,' Ember called.

Naturally, this twitchy sod never expected Harpur and Iles to show and kept saying they wouldn't at the pre-meal bar. The pair arrived just as guests were going into the dining room, and then Ember wanted to be a full, gorgeous part of the triumph, of course. Ralphy had always behaved like this – how he got that big country house, Low Pastures, and the paddock and everything, as well as the Monty layabouts' club. Ember knew how to wait until he saw how things were going, and if it turned bad he'd scamper fast. But if it looked good, he'd join and pretend he'd been right into it all along. This was a fine skill, Manse would never deny that, and the scamper side had brought Ember his sticky title, Panicking Ralph or Panicking Ralphy.

'Thank you, indeed, for this charming welcome, Manse,' Iles said. He had sat down again. 'It's been one of the best villain meals I've ever tasted, and the wines definitely one-up from gut rot. I don't know whether Harpur shares my appreciation. He eats out with crud a lot more than I do and may have seen better spreads.'

'What it seemed to me and Ralph,' Manse replied, 'was a proper *occasion* had to be laid on as a sort of symbol – similar to certain diplomatic dinners arranged to show what's known as "bonding" with a foreign leader, black or white or even yellow, or, of course, the Last Supper. Now, look, I don't say Mr Iles and Mr Harpur are our *colleagues* all at once, just because it's three strikes for cannabis before a punter's done. That would be crazy. Police officers must keep their own very separate little roles and identities. There got to be what's often termed decorum.' He paused and looked around the table to make sure everyone knew this word. 'Yes, decorum, or acting proper. Big police must go very careful, as ever – known as keeping their nose clean, and I don't mean just from coke. Being sort of pure – that's what I mean. What I'm saying is that by being here tonight Mr Iles and Mr Harpur are not telling us the trade is now one hundred per cent legit, no way. They're telling us blind-eyeing's on the up. Now, admitted, we've had blind-eyeing for many a good month under Mr Iles, who sort of invented the blind eye, the way God or Nature – what you fancy – the way whichever invented the *good* eyes. This was a grand creation by Mr Iles, like Whittle and the jet engine. But now the blind-eyeing is even blinder and it's official, meaning it starts not just from Mr Desmond Iles but from above him, there being some above Mr Iles, although you would never of thought it, the style he got with his hair and jokes and clothing and shoes.'

'Thanks, Manse,' Iles replied. 'Obviously, I have to make

sure I'm never considered as being at the same rather undeveloped level as Harpur in the style aspect. But he's improving. I'm glad you mentioned those above me. Oh, yes, they *do* exist. They have their tragic, small, extremely well-meant ideas – of course they do – it's expected of them – what they are paid for – and their self-respect demands they come out with something now and then, however dreamy. I like many of these people. They can't be called harmless exactly, but malice certainly does not figure. However, it would be sloppy to think of such folk as altogether in touch with things as things really are. After all, these are politicians, or are officers who have *pleased* politicians and earned promotion, so you can see we are not necessarily dealing with unimpaired minds, poor, poor worthies.'

Shale had told one of his people to prepare a flip-chart and left his place at the head of the table and walked over now to where it waited on a stand. Manse thought of himself as a flip-chart kind of person. Things in life could be vague and complicated – he certainly recognized this – but with a flip-chart you could bring some definition. Important philosophers in academic buildings discussing large topics like the meaning of light, or the shape of thought, would definitely find help in a flip-chart. Manse presented the first page of his now to the folk seated around the long dining board with their port or brandy. He liked the movement when you used a flip-chart – that turning of the blank cover back to reveal a perfect idea or two. This showed like generosity because you would share the ideas by displaying them, no hoarding. But also the action of flipping the sheets up had punch to it, told folk you'd got matters into shape for them. The page showed:

ENTERPRISE
CO-OPERATION
ORDER

Manse had asked to have them set out in this way, like

90

a column, a strong column, offering support. He said:
'I think these have been our key words until recently, and
grand key words they are.' He flipped over to page 2. This
had

ENTERPRISE

divided very clearly into its components via arrows lead-
ing from this main word:

a. *Expanding sales force*
b. *Expanding customer base*
c. *Special Markets*

And then *Special Markets* was itself divided up into,
*universities, colleges, jails, barristers' chambers, touring theatre
and ballet groups, bridge clubs, golf clubs, raves, aerobic centres,
local government offices, unisex hairdressers.*
Following pages added details likewise to their central
themes:

CO-OPERATION

was divided into

a. *mutual recognition and respect of turf areas*
b. *commodity prices standard from firm to firm*
c. *agreed grievance procedures*
d. *graded disciplinary measures financial and other*

ORDER

listed

a. *street peace resulting from CO-OPERATION (see previous
page)* He liked that way of what was known as cross-
referencing. It proved system and unity.
b. *two-way consideration between firms and Law and vice
versa*

c. absolute firearms ban for all staff while dealing
d. strong discouragement of all weaponry for all staff while dealing including knives and garrotting wire
e. recognition that officers might occasionally have to bring 'show' prosecutions despite two-way consideration mentioned above

Manse took the meeting through these themes, pointing with a special stick. At the end he said: 'Now, what we got to recognize is some of this could be only history because of certain changes you all know of. What we got to work out tonight is how many of these various factors are still all right regardless.' He exposed the next chart page. Manse made sure he did this with some slowness and respect. It was not a flip but more solemn, like unveiling a war memorial. This sheet contained the names of the four Stave Street dead:

DONALD WADE SANGSTER-THAME
BERNARD HUGH MORETON
FRANK CALHOUN
CLEMENT LISS VAYLING

Shale said: 'I got to ask – we all got to ask – what happened to order? Where've it gone to? Can we ever bring it back?' On the four subsequent pages, each name had capital letter presentation and was then given back-up detail, like *ENTERPRISE, CO-OPERATION* and *ORDER*.

DONALD WADE SANGSTER-THAME
Age: 44.
Physical appearance: 5' 11", slight build, dark hair receding.
Career: Established minor-scale dealer handling all commodities. Previously operating for Ferdinand Dubal (deceased.) Recently acting independently, perhaps aiming to build own firm.
Vehicle: Laguna, third hand.
Wardrobe: Non-suit. Bargain shop jeans. Denim jacket. Dark T-shirts. Suede boots.

Home situation: No children. Lived with non-user, non-dealer Adrienne (Ady) Carmichael, comprehensive school teacher, Mill Wheel, Norman Road, Religious Knowledge and PE. Address: 8b Egremont Street – four room, first floor flat. Rent £370 a month
Family of origin: Father, the Rev. Peter Sidney Sangster-Thame, Church of England rector. Mother active in charities. Brother, Gregory, garden clearances. Sister, Veronica, tour guide.

Suddenly, a woman said from the other end of the Agincourt dinner table: 'Interesting, Mr Shale, and beautifully laid out but he's dead, isn't he? Do we want to be stuck with the past? All right, his mother's active in charities. I'm a mother. I understand about mothers, but so? We want the future, don't we?'

Manse certainly did not mind women attending the Agincourt meetings, even women this old. Obviously, women worked for the firms and it would have been poor to shut them out of the dinners. Manse hated sexism of any kind whatsoever, but who the fuck let this mouthy bitch in?

She was standing down near the bottom left bit of the table, alongside Bart Haverson, a long-time pusher who worked inside the Ralphy firm. Christ, Bart had a mother? Christ, Bart had a mother who pushed? 'You said yourself, Mr Shale, that some aspects of those big, big words, Enterprise, Co-operation, Order, might be out of date,' she said. 'Should we trouble ourselves with them, then? Shouldn't we change, adapt, advance?'

'My God, Manse, that suit!' Iles said. 'Where did it come from, the Lloyd George Museum?'

'Madam,' Shale replied, 'I'm afraid I don't know your –'

'Delphine Haverson,' she said.

'Mrs Haverson, for me, and for many similar, I think, the past can in many respects cast its light forward to reveal the future,' Shale said.

'That mean anything? Let's skip the flip-chart, I'd like us to drink a toast,' she replied. 'Two toasts. One to Ralph

Ember. The other to Detective Chief Superintendent Colin Harpur. They, *they*, have brought us our wondrous tomorrows.'

'Don't worry about cutting me out of that,' Iles yelled at her.

Shale, standing by his flip-chart, felt the meeting slide from him, felt his whole status slide. Those fucking instincts he had such a stack of told him he was all at once into catastrophe. 'Toasts?' he said. 'Toasts, I regret, would hardly be appropriate at this actual juncture. Hardly at all. We are engaged in a business presentation.'

'Toasts why?' she replied. 'I mean, exactly why? You're entitled to ask. Certainly you are.'

'The why don't come into it in the least, I fear,' Shale said. 'Just total unsuitability. Remember when I was mentioning decorum just now? That's what we got to have now. I'm sure others in the meeting familiar with what's called protocol will agree. Protocol is just like decorum – vital in a commercial setting.' The Heckler and Koch was heavy in his pocket. It did not comfort him. It made him feel slobbish, like he could only do cordite blast-offs, like he was lost if a scene went subtle. He had been looking out for a blood-and-gun plot against him between Denz and Ralphy. But maybe that's not how it would happen. A gang of them wanted to destroy him, yes, and probably Denz and Ember were included. They would do it by smart-arse talk and argument, though, like Parliament or a proper, straight-up business company. They'd found some dandruffed, shapeless slag in leathers to piss on him, bringing extra insult. How could a mother be so harsh, even Bart Haverson's mother?

This fucker Iles might be in on it – dishonouring Shale's selected garments like that in public, trying to drag him down, break his dignity, through ignorant, cruel lip, so typical. Iles, the proud lout, thought nobody but himself knew tailoring. But Manse would bet Iles didn't understand shit about the history of lapels or the lovely quality of older buttons. It hurt Mansel to hear someone knock a flip-chart. Chaos must be near. Execution – this was what they aimed for, just like with that famed English king many centuries ago up wood steps to where everyone could see his head come off. Now, they would not use an axe, only the worse wounds from words.

'So, you ask, why a toast to Ralph? I'll tell you,' she said. 'Exultation at the Valencia. Peace at the Valencia. Order at the Valencia. No, it has not disappeared, Mr Shale. It has been accomplished. And now we have a future at the Valencia. Four dead, three locked up. Who fixed it? No official statement on that, yet. No flip-chart entry in big, fat capital letters. But don't we all know a whisper went in the right direction? Don't we all know where that educated whisper came from? Ladies and gentlemen, I give you Ralph W. Ember, his fine name to be coupled with that of Mr Colin Harpur, our second toast, who heard the whisper and made his brilliantly calculated, Stave Street, solo response.'

Chapter Six

'Many believe it was a really prime bit of solo work by you, dad.'

'Which many?' Harpur replied.

'At school,' Jill said.

'She means kids,' Hazel said.

'Prime,' Jill said.

'In what way?' Harpur asked.

'This is how they're talking down there,' Jill replied.

'Down where?' Harpur asked.

'I told you – school,' Jill said. 'The buzz.'

'The *buzz*,' Hazel said. 'Kids like that, youngsters – they catch up on words a century after they're dead. Who says buzz now?'

'What buzz?' Harpur asked.

'Meaning information passed on,' Jill said.

'Which information?' Harpur said.

'You – down the Valencia that night,' Jill replied. 'Some information comes from the media, obviously. But some inside stuff.'

'What inside stuff?' Hazel said. 'How do snotty kids get inside stuff?'

'Yes, some inside stuff,' Jill said.

'Which inside stuff?' Harpur asked.

'Sort of passed on. There's a phrase for it called "word of mouth",' Jill said.

'My! Is that right?' Hazel replied. 'There are phrases for everything these days. I can't keep up.'

'But where does it come from?' Harpur asked.

'The rumour factory,' Hazel said.

'They say you were brilliant,' Jill replied.

'Who do?' Harpur asked.

'My friends,' Jill said.

'Kids,' Hazel said.

Jill said: 'Dad, I got to admit –'

'Have to admit,' Harpur said.

'I admit these are friends who don't *usually* say good things about the police,' Jill replied. 'But now – "brilliant".'

'I want you to be careful,' Harpur said.

'How d'you mean, careful?' Hazel asked.

'Eyes open,' Harpur replied.

'For what?' Hazel said.

'And such as letting people into the house when I'm not here,' Harpur said. 'Yes, careful.'

'You mean Mr Iles, because of Haze and her tendencies?' Jill asked.

'Bitch queen,' Hazel said.

'People you don't know,' Harpur replied.

'This because of what *she* said?' Hazel said.

'Look, these reports about the Valencia – they're not helpful,' Harpur said. 'Not true, not helpful.'

'Dangerous?' Hazel asked.

'The buzz?' Jill said.

'Dangerous how?' Hazel asked.

Jill said: 'But all the stuff I hear is *good*, dad. I told you, it says you –'

'Were brilliant,' Harpur said.

'How can that be dangerous?' Jill asked.

Harpur said: 'All I want is –'

'For us to be careful,' Hazel said.

'When they say brilliant they mean how you fixed it so some get knocked over, others inside. It's the *smartness* of it, dad,' Jill said. 'I got to admit . . . I *have* to admit they don't usually think of police as smart. They think of Inspector Knacker, like in *Private Eye*. Or PC Plod. They think it was really sharp and devilish to be down there arranging it all. Like a fair or running a pop concert.'

'Dad, how you going to explain that to the court?' Hazel asked. 'Obviously you were tipped off, but you let it

97

happen. Bullets everywhere. If you OK something like that, just allow it – is a court going to regard that as proper policing?'

'That's what I mean, smart,' Jill said.

'Some lawyer will bite bits out of you, dad,' Hazel said.

'Creeps,' Jill said. 'Lawyers. Who'd be one?'

'You're scared you'll get the blame for the killings and jailings and there could be a vengeance party now, today, tomorrow – never mind the court?' Hazel asked. 'That one, Vayling, who was shot – he's a big villain, yes? What the Press said. I expect he's got friends, has he? Family. Vendetta?'

'A fink told you it was all going to take place, did he? Or she?' Jill said.

'I've asked you not to talk TV before,' Harpur replied.

'What TV?' Jill asked.

'Fink,' Harpur said.

'A voice, then,' Jill replied.

'The court is bound to give you a rough time about that, isn't it, dad?' Hazel asked. 'Courts don't like informants.'

'I was there by fluke,' Harpur said. 'Simply patrolling my ground.'

'At school they said you'd say that,' Jill replied, 'because of the court and everything. That's part of the cleverness.'

'Which everything?' Harpur said.

'Vengeance,' Jill replied. 'Gang vengeance.'

'Just stay watchful,' Harpur said.

'Vengeance against *us*?' Jill said.

'There are big changes going on,' Harpur replied.

'Yes, that child,' Hazel said.

'Which?' Harpur asked.

'Burned,' Hazel replied. 'Lorraine Sambrook. Is that part of it?'

'What?' Harpur said.

'The change,' Hazel said.

'I'm going to see her mother at the hospital today,' Harpur replied. 'She's out of danger now.'

'Oh, poor, poor lady,' Hazel said.

'Does she *want* to see you?' Jill said.

'She asked for me,' Harpur replied.

'In person?' Jill said.

'Probably I'm the only police name she knows', Harpur said.

'In person – it could be important,' Jill replied. 'Well, be kind. No bullying. All that – oh, you know.'

'What?' Harpur asked.

'Keeping on at her – questions, more questions,' Jill said.

'Interrogation,' Hazel said.

'Aren't you the one for the big words, though?' Jill replied. 'And then Venetia Ember. Venetia! Where did that come from? You know, dad – Panicking Ralphy's daughter. Milord Monty.'

'What about her?' Harpur asked.

'Some girl in judo goes to that Corton school – private,' Jill said. 'He brought Venetia back from France. Was he worried about her out there – wants to keep an eye?'

'Is that what you mean – big changes?' Hazel asked. 'Dangerous all round?'

'My friends say you must of done some of the shooting yourself,' Jill said.

'Must have,' Harpur replied.

'You did?' Jill asked. 'You're telling us you did?'

'No. It's must *have*, not must *of*,' Harpur said.

'She can't help it,' Hazel said. 'She's a retard.'

'They like that, too,' Jill replied.

'What?' Harpur said.

'The shooting,' Jill said. 'What kind of piece? Like true police work. Not just nicking people for joy rides. The people killed – only pushers. If they can't take a joke they shouldn't have joined.'

'You know I don't carry a firearm,' Harpur replied.

'Sometimes you do,' Jill said.

'Hardly ever,' Harpur replied.

'I think you should,' Jill said. 'It helps you seem more . . . well, grown up. It would make those suits you wear not so bad if people knew you had a gun under them. They'd think the scruffiness and the way they don't fit right is to get enemies into a lull because you look so shambolic, and no pistol bulge when the clothes hang off of you loose, like disguise. And you'd be safer. Denise would want you to carry something, in case you get blasted and are gone. You should think about her, left behind. This is a girl, still young and beautiful, and yet she doesn't seem to worry about your haircut and age and music. All right, she got a brain and boobs and she'd find somebody else, but she'd be upset for a while. And then, what about us?'

'Who?' Harpur asked.

'Hazel and I.'

'Hazel and me,' Harpur said.

'No, I mean Hazel and I,' Jill said. '*You* might be dead.'

'It's Hazel and *me*,' Harpur said. '"What about Hazel and me?" I'd like it better if you didn't talk to people outside about guns.'

'Denise isn't a person outside,' Jill replied.

'Your friends,' Harpur said.

'You're afraid the word will get around you shot people at the Valencia?' Hazel asked. 'And so a vengeance posse, definitely?'

'It's inaccurate, that's all,' Harpur said. 'I've told you, I don't carry a firearm.'

'People in school said you'd say that,' Jill replied, 'because it would look like a dirty ambush otherwise. This was a true operation, dad. I'm really proud.'

'So gracious of you,' Hazel said.

Yes, Vayling would be someone to worry about and, driving to St Mary's Hospital now, Harpur worried about him. Mansel Shale's flip-chart at the Agincourt Hotel had eventually reached Vayling's name and CV, despite the interruption from Bart Haverson's mother, and those other, louder interruptions. You could not expect Iles to sit through a meeting of that type without being provoked into some kind of showy convulsions. Shale's page had said:

CLEMENT LISS VAYLING
Age: 50.
Physical appearance: 6' 1", 210lb, bald.
Career: Trainee chef. Teenage burglary convictions. Bouncer,
minder roles 1997–8. Enforcer, debt-collector, pusher 1998–,
Hull, Harrogate, Liverpool, London. Two possible murders in
turf disputes, Peckham, London. Also woundings, Peckham,
Liverpool, Manchester. Handgun proficient – Walther?
Vehicle: Various.
Wardrobe: Hand-made dark suits. Black high-grade lace-up
shoes.
Home situation: Long-term male partner, Christopher Tobias
Ophus, age 31, professional classical musician – timpani.
Addresses: 19 Great Park Close, Milldale, Liverpool. E4 Bate's
Caravan Park, New Cross, London.
Family of origin: Father, self-employed builder, Liverpool
(dead). Mother, maiden name Liss, remarried and untraceable.
Two brothers. Leonard, a primary school headmaster, Surrey,
Graham, tabloid newspaper sub-editor, London.

At the Agincourt, Manse Shale had offered profiles of all
four Valencia dead. Delphine Haverson's questions about
relevance could not stop him. There was a picture to
provide, and Manse meant to provide it. He obviously
thought his whole credibility as a business leader required
him to go on. Harpur sympathized. Manse had created a
status for himself over years, and flip-charts helped build
it. Thoroughness was one of Shale's most prized qualities,
a quality he could not let slip on account of someone's
apprentice pusher mother.

It was Haverson himself who stupidly set Iles off in full
Iles style and Iles duration at the Agincourt meet. But
Harpur saw it might be unfair to blame Bart totally. You
needed to know Iles as well as Harpur did to forecast what
exactly would bring on one of the Assistant Chief's massive, gorgeous fits. Haverson used the same kind of argument as his mother. All right, yes, Manse, Vayling had
been a foul, professional menace. But had *been*. Had been,
had been, had been. Now he was removed. And his

101

removal would warn others who might have looked in this direction and hoped to extend their game here. How, then, had this fine result been achieved, with its grand implications about future trade tranquillity at the Valencia? Nobody knew the full answer to that, but he, Bart, had certain ideas – in fact, certain certainties! There had been some intelligent pre-planning. There had been some brilliant pre-knowledge. That pre-knowledge, as he saw things, came from one of the most distinguished members at their banquet tonight, Ralph W. Ember. Haverson had paused for a moment, as if expecting Ember to stand and acknowledge the grand applause that followed mention of his name. But Ralph remained seated, his face impassive, strong, very El Cid.

Haverson started again. Who had Ralph passed that fine pre-knowledge to? Could there be even the most minor doubt? How did Detective Chief Superintendent Colin Harpur contrive to be at the scene of these health-bringing deaths, and thus able to orchestrate not only them, but also the subsequent arrest of those who survived the timely Valencia cleansing? Answer obvious, Bart said. This had been an operation of majestic design and implementation, its benefits long-term and vast. As folk would have seen, these benefits brought a new zest to his mother, and perhaps to others' mothers, even to the extent that she now contemplated a fresh career – as some in their maturity turned away from, say, stockbroking and recognized a vocation for teaching or the Church. Listening to the haywire and perilous praise for his supposed role in the killings and possible jail sentences, Harpur had felt a rising rush of goose vomit but just kept it more or less back.

Iles had stood up before Bart properly finished and talked over him. The Assistant Chief said he naturally delighted to hear Harpur praised. This was a man who, although living in Arthur Street, had quite authentic ambitions for himself and for his two daughters. Commendation such as they'd just heard from Bart would lift Harpur's little soul and bring it up towards normality. That was worthwhile progress. Harpur chewed on flattery the way cows chewed the cud, and his juices needed it. As to his juices, many of them would probably be wondering how he could talk so amiably about him now when it was no time since he was putting it to Iles's wife in various unwholesome and sometimes hazardous settings. The ACC's voice crackled a bit and grew louder but Harpur could see no froth around his mouth yet. Some people there would have watched these kinds of performance from Iles in the past, and everyone would have heard of them. They were par. And yet, Iles went on, not always unwholesome settings. Now and then, as he understood it, when he was away from home, Harpur would actually come to the Assistant Chief's house, Idylls, in Rougemont Place, on the quiet and through the garden, but spotted by a neighbour, or how would he, Iles, know? Iles considered it most likely Harpur felt a true thrill to be allowed into this property and district after the Arthur Street silt.

'Many's the conversation Mr Iles and I have about social class as revealed by local geog,' Harpur had said.

So – Iles continued – this Agincourt meeting would see he expected no openness or simple honesty from Harpur. Those attending might have assumed that because Iles was his superior, he, the ACC, might have been told of the scenario Harpur had for the Valencia that killing night. Negative. As ever, Harpur went his own secretive way. Iles said he understood Harpur's purpose was to secure commercial peace.

'Hear, hear,' Haverson said.

Iles smiled and walked around the table, put his hand under Ralph Ember's coat and brought out a 9 mm Beretta automatic. He checked the working and put the gun on the table. Then Iles went to where Shale had sat down again after the flip-chart session and lifted another 9 mm automatic from his jacket pocket, a Heckler and Koch. Iles admired the lines of this and placed it alongside Ember's pistol. Afterwards, the ACC took a few more steps and removed from each of Denzil Lake's coat pockets a short-barrelled Astra Modelo .38 revolver. Iles posed with both pointing out into the room, like a Wild West actor. In a moment he set these Astras with the other two weapons.

Harpur could recall the rest of the talk verbatim, especially his own protest. 'Did you say peace?' Iles asked, gazing at the dinner table arsenal. 'This is peace? How lovely. How guaranteed.' He went back to his chair.

'Just adornment,' Mrs Haverson yelled, 'like jewellery or a headband. Why nit-pick at this happy juncture?'

'Peace? I, I, I, Desmond Iles, was peace,' he said. 'I embodied peace and peace embodied me. Now, no longer. Harpur, fucking one's wife in one's fine villa, and, most probably, in bed-bug hotels, in cars, in multiplex cinema lavatories – or Harpur laying on a back street massacre with Ralphy's aid – it's the same – the inauguration of chaos. We have it with us now. Weep. This is his unique septic flair.'

'No,' Harpur had cried, 'no. I didn't lay on the massacre. Impossible, do you hear, all of you?'

'But what about the rest of it?' Iles screamed.

'Which rest of it?' Harpur said.

Iles said: 'In one's villa, in mucky hotels, in –'

'Oh, God, sir, does place matter?' Harpur replied.

'Not chaos,' Mrs Haverson called. 'Splendid, glittering promise. Please, please, recognize it and rejoice.'

'Which multiplex?' Iles yelled. 'What had you seen? It sickens me to think of her watching a film with you, Harpur. So chummy and flagrant. Was it a comedy you saw? You damn well *guffawed* together? My God.'

At St Mary's Hospital, Harpur wondered if the doctors had it right and Curly Sambrook's girlfriend, Charlotte Ivens, really was out of danger. She looked frighteningly broken and weak. Perhaps the doctors meant physical damage no longer threatened. But they might also see that other injuries tore at her mind and morale, made her reluctant to take on life in full again. Possibly they had let her send for Harpur now, hoping this was something positive, a willingness to talk about the fire, not keep those memories unspilled and undiluted, destructive inside her. One side of her face was disfigured and would always be disfigured – replacement skin shining, and too smooth and pink. This was a woman of, what, twenty-eight, twenty-nine, and stuck with that for keeps? She wore a high-necked, long-sleeved nightdress and white close-fitting linen hat, so he could not tell how else she had been burned. But, of course, he knew it had been almost as catastrophic as for Curly and their daughter. She was still in bed and kept her hands under the covers. Talking was a labour to her, but it gave her pleasure, too, he saw that. She wanted to smile now and then, but the way they'd organized her face did not allow this fully. She had a private room. He sat in a basketwork armchair.

'Thanks for visiting,' she said.

'You're doing so well.'

'They say.'

'It's true.'

'I saw about the Valencia. Even when I was bad I could watch some television,' she replied. There was a set in the corner above her bed.

'Yes, a rough episode.'

'I liked it. I wanted them to let me invite you before this, but they wouldn't.'

'They have to be careful.'

'To thank you,' she replied.

'Oh, there's nothing to –'

'That fucker, Vayling,' she said. 'You got the fucker.' Although her lips had lost some stretch she popped the swearword out well each time, gave it true thoroughness and dwelt on the mid-consonants.

A nurse came in and said: 'Not more than five minutes, Charlotte.'

'I'm all right.'

'Not more than five minutes,' the nurse said. This time she addressed Harpur. He nodded. The nurse left.

Charlotte said: 'When I was bad – worse – that's what kept me going, you know.'

'What?'

'You got the fucker.'

'Well, I –'

105

'I don't say you did it yourself, not pulled the trigger. But impresario. I was scared I'd go under for keeps and not have time to say thanks. That's what I mean – it kept me going. It still does. I was drugged up, of course, but I'd come out of it now and then and alongside the pain the thought would always arrive that I must get my gratitude to you. I felt it would be a terrible failure if I died without letting you know. This was so smart what you did, Mr Harpur, so fine – such a good thing for Curly and Lorraine as well as myself.'

Smart. It was eerie to hear Jill's word. Here, though, it would be wrong to deny he'd shown smartness. Charlotte Ivens depended at least a bit on her belief in it and him. Her joy at Vayling's death and Harpur's apparent role in it was part of the treatment. 'This will sound foolish, I expect, but I feel you should try to think about yourself more now, about recovery,' Harpur replied. 'You've come along brilliantly, and you must go on like that. I'm sure Curly and Lorraine would wish that, wouldn't they?'

'You decided Vayling would never be caught for what he did, torching the house – no evidence. The fucker got away with all sorts before this. So you did him your own way. Unofficial but justice. Often justice needs some help. That really gave me rapture and strength when I saw it on the News and heard you were actually there. It goes on giving me rapture and strength. It makes me believe things could still be all right, or close to all right, because there are people like you. Vayling – he hears Curly has a nice little business corner going and growing and he wants it. Where he came from, all he had to do was say he wanted something and that was it. Not Curly. He wasn't one to step aside. And so – well, everyone knows what came next. And that could have been the end of it, but for you.'

'Some thought Curly might have –'

'Been a grass? My mother said she'd heard that – when she came in. Curly, never. Wouldn't you know if he had been? You're ringmaster to the grasses, aren't you? No, just market-fucking-forces – your traditional free trade competition, plus a firebomb.'

The nurse reappeared. Harpur stood.

'Thank you, thank you, Mr Harpur,' Charlotte said. 'He got that fucker, Vayling, you know, Amy.'

'I think you've really done Charlotte a lot of good today,' the nurse said.

'You're very kind,' Harpur replied.

'Isn't he great, Amy? Such lovely politeness but it's the same man who can go out and do a fucker like Vayling.'

Harpur kissed her on the linen hat. 'Keep fighting,' he said.

'And you. Will you get trouble?'

'Which?' Harpur asked.

'With the Law, the courts,' she replied. 'Won't they want to know how you came to be there, running things? If my hands are all right by then I'll write a character reference for you to the judge. I'll say only someone through-and-through good would recognize a duty to get that fucker, Vayling.'

When Harpur reached home, Denise was with the children and they had a guest. 'I know you told us not to let anyone in, dad,' Jill said, 'but, look, he's a vicar – well, we thought vicars would be safe because of their holy side. All right, the front door glass is not proper see-through but we could tell it was a dog collar. He was under the porch light, with a good shine off of the collar. And he seemed too tall to be Mr Iles dressed up, trying to get in by a wangle. We asked Denise and she decided vicars would be all right as long as it was a genuine vicar, not, say, some hit-man pretending to be a vicar, which would be quite easy, admitted.'

'Admittedly,' Harpur replied.

Jill said: 'I asked Denise how to tell if it was only someone *pretending* to be a vicar and she came out into the hall with us and had a look at him. She said about the shine off of the dog collar, too. And when we opened the door, but before we let him in, Denise asked what it was about, such as charity collecting or aerobics in the church hall, and then she decided he probably was a real vicar because not a scar anywhere and this harvest festival voice

– what she called it, meaning like smooth but loud enough, I think. He told us he had to see you.'

'This is the Rev. Peter Sidney Sangster-Thame,' Hazel said.

'He's the dad of that Donald Wade Sangster-Thame sadly killed in Stave Street,' Jill said. 'Some might not think a vicar would have a son like that, but that's what "the black sheep of the family" means. All right, Donald was only a small-time peddler, but his father could still be upset about him. This is how families are, they care about even the villain, even the nobody villain. We've checked identity through his driver's licence and a credit card. He's straight up, a Rev.'

'I feel entitled to the truth about my son's death, Mr Harpur,' Sangster-Thame said.

'I told him you're often one for the real truth, dad,' Jill said, 'unless lies can't be avoided, of course, because of the job.'

'I've gone over the detail of it with him, as in the Press and on TV,' Hazel said, 'but this is not what Mr Sangster-Thame means. He knows all that.'

'His question is, was it a set-up?' Jill asked.

'Scenarioed,' Hazel said.

'My friends at school think it was, obviously, and they love it,' Jill said. 'But someone's father might not be so pleased. I can understand that, for definite. What the Rev. could regard his son as when shot like that is a sacrifice. Someone like the Rev. who does a lot with the Bible would often be thinking about sacrifices, such as Isaac nearly stabbed by his own father in Genesis, although Donald Wade Sangster-Thame was much older.'

'As I understand it, this was an operation devised to wipe out a certain targeted criminal regardless of what other loss of life might be entailed,' Sangster-Thame said. 'I do not *wish* to believe this, but am compelled.' He was over six feet, heavily made, long-faced, about sixty-two. Harpur admired him for digging away. A father could never let go. Harpur recognized that if you left your name and address in the phone book, people would come calling. That was why he had warned the girls. But he felt it right the public should know how to reach him. He saw streaks of egomania in Sangster-Thame's meaty features – the push of the jaw and occasional proud pout. That would be normal for someone used to browbeating congregations. He had to get a myth across.

'Possibly I should speak to Mr Sangster-Thame alone briefly,' Harpur said.

'Clement Liss Vayling, main man,' Jill replied. 'Liss was his mother's maiden name. This is well known, via the News.'

'The Press reckoned Vayling was a killer, even before he arrived here,' Hazel said. 'But somehow unnailed. It happens. There are people who can buy out of trouble.'

They were in Harpur's big sitting room. One of the girls or Denise had made tea. Hazel handed around the cups from a tray. Jill at the table cut slices from a chocolate cake, then distributed these on smaller plates. The others sat in armchairs.

'My son and those with him, Morcton, Calhoun – simply bait?' Sangster-Thame asked.

'Colin would never be party to anything like that,' Denise said. It was instant, flat, sweeping.

'I'm sorry. You are?' Sangster-Thame said, turning towards her. 'Your role here is?'

'As a matter of fact, I could see you wondered about Denise,' Jill replied. She leaned back against the table and gazed at the ceiling, doing some reflection. 'Denise is young but not as young as us, well, obviously. Dad and Denise – it's a really lovely thing, although she's young and in university. This has been going on for ever so many months. This is really mature.'

'We've given it the OK,' Hazel said.

'Very much so,' Jill said.

'We don't regard Denise as totty,' Hazel said.

'Denise is not exactly a live-in because some nights she sleeps at the student residences after partying or French poetry revision, including one "It rains in my heart" that she told me about, but she's here often and it's great when

109

we all have breakfast together, nearly how it used to be,' Jill said. 'Our mother was murdered, you know.* Oh, yes. That was very bad. It rained in *my* heart then. Dad's got rid of all her books out of this room, except a couple I wanted. I think dad and Denise already had some togetherness going before my mother died. I don't suppose a vicar likes hearing this. Mum and dad were both that way. They did look around. It's through being brought up in the 1960s and '70s. Sex was everywhere. Mr Sangster-Thame, if you already wanted to be a vicar even then, perhaps you didn't notice, but it's well known in history, called social change.'

'Of course, I regretted the life Donald had chosen,' Sangster-Thame said, 'especially as his brother and sister have such . . . but leave that . . . they have their careers and he, I suppose, would claim to have had his, and I will not dwell on comparisons. All are, or were, my dear children.'

'It's important children get treated the same,' Jill replied. 'Dad's quite good at that, although Hazel gives him grief, because of a senior officer called Iles. You wouldn't think he was police. He's got a crimson scarf and it doesn't seem to bother him about still under-age.'

'Shut up, sheep dung,' Hazel said.

'Let me only acknowledge that I prayed for Donald,' Sangster-Thame said. 'I prayed for the three of them, but for Donald more. Yes, considerably more. I asked that he might leave that awful trade and find something wholesome, above board. One had to believe this was possible. I *did* believe it possible, as priest and parent. This is the Christian hope – that no one is for ever lost. There is redemption. And perhaps the change would have happened one day.'

'Dad went to Sunday School a lot when he was small,' Jill replied. 'He knows all that about redemption and the thief on the cross, for instance.'

Sangster-Thame said: 'But then, suddenly, this terrible,

* *Roses, Roses*

110

almost offhand death. The police had a plan, didn't they? You, Mr Harpur, had a plan. This is how it looks. You – present in the street to make sure things went as you wanted. There was one objective – create the setting for a gun battle in which a formidable, defiant public enemy might be removed, so achieving what the legal forces of this country had never been able to do. And to further this project, other lives were casually, coldly put at risk. I had prayed to God that my son might emerge from the degradations of the drugs trade. Instead, he is wiped out as an insignificant extra in a ruthless, bold, lawless operation to destroy someone else. Mr Harpur, if my version is right, this must annihilate the very basis of my faith – do you see? Oh, do you not see?' He put his arms and hands forward as though reaching for reassurance, one hand holding a teacup. 'Well, you may say that this is not your problem, but mine.'

'Colin doesn't talk like that,' Denise replied.

'She'll always stand up for him, you see,' Jill said. 'This is how it should be in a relationship. One thing I'm sure you've heard of, Mr Sangster-Thame, is empathy.'

He said: 'It is not that my prayers have been rejected. One would accept this. Only some prayers can succeed. But it is as if there is nobody there to hear them – as if circumstances, events, have their own unthinking drive and power, destroying at random.'

'Existentialism,' Denise said.

'No God. A void,' Sangster-Thame replied. 'Where am I? Where is my church?' Harpur felt sympathy for him. Sangster-Thame had plenty of phoniness and noise like any minister of any religion anywhere, but this confusion seemed real and touching.

'Existentialism,' Denise said, 'yes. Things happen because someone perhaps unknowingly makes them happen. There's no big, benign system – no system at all. Everything's ad hoc and probably bad.'

Harpur watched Jill think about this for a time. The word 'existentialism' would block her. It blocked Harpur.

111

Denise could turn intellectual and damn showy sometimes. Harpur put up with it. Education did matter. Then
Jill said: 'Look, your Donald's pal Bernie carried a piece,
didn't he, Mr Sangster-Thame? It was in the Press. Someone with a piece packs a piece because he thinks he's going
to meet someone else with a piece. That's just logical. So,
gunning is nearly certain to come. I don't know what you
mean, Denise, when you say no system. That what you
said? There *is* a system. It's who shoots first stays OK. If
dad laid it all on, that's a system, too. The system was to
get as many of them as could be got. I'm sorry about
Donald, Mr Sangster-Thame, but that was the game he
picked, wasn't it?' She moved away from the table and
took Sangster-Thame another slice of cake in her fingers.

Harpur said: 'No plan. Chance. I was there by
chance.'

In bed later when Sangster-Thame had gone and the
children slept Denise said: 'That's even worse for him.'

'What?' Harpur asked.

'Chance. Luck.'

'Yes. Yes? How?'

'Luck is chaos,' Denise replied.

'Iles is always on about chaos lately.'

'Sangster-Thame prays for his boy, asks God kindly to
rearrange Donald's life in the New Testament pattern of
salvation from sin, and believes it could happen. With
time, it might have. But there *is* no time. Along comes an
event out of nowhere and sees Donald off. The Rev. thinks
you're responsible. You say you only saw it by fluke.
Doesn't matter. It's at least chaos and maybe godly
spite.'

'I see Curly's Charlotte in hospital and let her believe
I fixed Stave Street and had Vayling killed. It's crucial – to
keep her interested in life. Therapy. Then I meet Sangster-
Thame and he wants to send me to hell for fixing the Stave
Street massacre and causing Donald's death before he
could be reclaimed.'

'What's true depends on where you're looking at it
from,' Denise replied. 'You haven't only just discovered

112

that, have you? And you a cop. Think how stories from the witness box clash with one another.'

Harpur groaned. 'Oh, God, the witness box. I'll have to give the story about Stave Street from there myself later on.'

'The true story?'

'Iles says truth is what the jury believes.'

'So, will they believe you?'

'They owned their house, you know.'

'Who?'

'Curly and the girl,' Harpur said.

'So?'

'A boy we met on the Ernest Bevin obviously thought we were all pretty much the same – Curly, Iles, myself – because we each had what he called "property".'

'You've always said that, anyway, haven't you?'

'What?'

'Not much difference between *them* and you,' Denise replied.

'Luck.'

'Things happen,' she said. 'No system.'

'You were grand tonight, defending me to Sangster-Thame,' Harpur replied.

'What else would I do?'

'Yes, what else would you do?'

'Now?'

'Now seems a good time,' he said.

'This?'

'Nice,' he replied.

'And what else would *you* do?' she asked.

'This?'

'For starters.'

Chapter Seven

Ralph Ember felt good. It came from more than trade boost possibilities in the dinner later tonight with Sashaying Vernon. An all-round, general contentment touched Ralph lately. Prestige seemed to dog him. There were small plus points, and much bigger ones. He noted what he'd definitely term deference from the head at Corton House school when he negotiated Venetia's re-enrolment. The lump of fees money he coughed in advance would not be the whole reason. No, Corton's principal evidently found his remarks on theatre impressive. He was glad he'd put a number of play titles in, showing range. What a difference here from that Bordeaux bitch. Ralph always responded well if treated properly. As he sometimes expressed it to himself with a flash of word-play, he appreciated being appreciated.

Again, it might seem insignificant to others, but he loved how when that vain slob, Iles, decided to search people for weapons at the Agincourt Hotel he took Ralph first. Iles was the sort to detect who had a gun aboard, or guns. This was more than a police nose. This was Iles his fucking self. All right, he got round to the others eventually – Manse and Denzil – but he picked Ralph for openers. Ember saw respect in that. He saw a fine, wholesome regard for precedence, for a formidable status. Iles did not think of him as Panicking Ralph, did he? Would he give top attention to a flake?

Ralph liked the way Iles had obviously admired his Beretta and enjoyed checking it. He didn't do this with either of the other two's weapons. It was almost as though

Iles knew that if Ralph were tooled up it would be with a beautiful gun in sweet condition. Some guns looked what they were and nothing else – bullet-flingers. The Beretta had lines, brave grace, style.

True, in a sense Assistant Chief Iles had wanted to make an utterly hostile point by exposing these pistols and piling them up like accusations on the long table. He was saying, wasn't he, that suspicions and potential aggression in the commercial context must always exist, no matter how sunny things appeared? But Iles would consider this so obvious it didn't need proving. The real message to reach all in the meeting must be that Iles recognized Ralph as far and away the most accomplished and worthwhile guest present, a sort of touchstone. Ember did not see any sexual motive – Iles using the gun search to get his hand inside Ralph's suit and on to his body around the tit area. Ember had certainly grown used to that kind of flesh interest from women and accepted it without quibble, regardless of the woman's looks, age and even dress sense. They would not be hunting a gun, of course, but simply wanted to touch him in a personal manner, especially those who saw his resemblance to the young Charlton Heston – all that chest in *Ben Hur* when he's rowing a galley. To Ember, it always seemed simply polite to put up with these pushy lusts in women. A man had duties. Kindness was an imperative with him when possible.

However, he would be astonished if Iles went anything but hetero, and Ralph thought the same almost undoubtedly true of himself. Although some said guns were cock symbols, Ralph did not deduce at all that for Iles to linger over his Beretta and jerk the working parts suggested an approach. The phrase 'tooled up' might create confusion. To frisk Ember early merely acknowledged him supremo. What else could Iles have done among that lot at the Agincourt, for God's sake? Supremo was what Ralph blatantly was. Mrs Delphine Haverson certainly saw this. She and Bart impressed Ralph. He might ease both up the hierarchy. Later tonight he'd probably drop in on them. Flux was certainly about. He had to take things gradually, bit by bit. So far, he'd put off telling Manse about Denzil. Shale had looked such an oaf at the Agincourt that possibly Denzil really was a better prospect.

Driving now towards the Grenoble restaurant, Ember thought he spotted a tail car – a red Volvo saloon. It hung back pretty cleverly and let a couple of other vehicles get between it and Ralph for cover on several sections of the trip. Then it would do some overtaking and come up close for a while. A man and woman sat in front, the woman driving. There might be someone else in the back. Ember had to do all his observations through the mirror and it was dark. It did not trouble him to be under surveillance. He expected that. This only echoed Iles's response at the Agincourt to Ralph's natural ranking. Probably Iles had ordered the Volvo crew to chart him. Or Iles might have told sidekick Harpur to order them. In the turmoil of developments now rocking the commercial scene, a major, wonderfully stable figure like Ralph became more than ever significant. Ralph Ember could understand that how Ralph Ember reacted to the changes would be a kind of beacon for them – an indication, and almost certainly the best indication, of the ways leadership in the firms might adjust. They would know that Ralph W. Ember did nothing without intelligent and intelligenced thought. He would be ahead of others in reading the new circumstances, but they would follow eventually, impressed as Iles was by the scope and positiveness of Ember's mind. He liked to speculate about how others saw him, or some others, anyway. It helped Ralph's attempts to plumb his identity. His identity, as a topic, fascinated him. He felt people who believed they knew absolutely who they were must be damn smug.

In a way, sharing his insights with Iles and Harpur seemed to Ralph another duty that fell uniquely on him, like the obligation to let women paw his physique and in some cases nuzzle into his neck, thrilled by contact with Ember's jaw scar, the excitable dears. He certainly did not mind these Volvo snoops noting that he went to meet Vernon. You couldn't eat at the Grenoble without word spreading, anyway. Iles and Harpur would realize this was the time for new alliances and fundamental new thinking. They must foresee that someone like Sashaying Vernon, possibly due a lot of jail, might want a partner on the outside to help him use the new favourable, blind-eye trading rules, so his family would not suffer an income drop, and so there'd be a good stack of cash for him on release. Such a partner would clearly have to be trustworthy and brilliantly capable in a business sense, and in staying unlocked up himself. Ember knew it was no big-headedness to see he fitted totally. Iles and Harpur might actually be *expecting* a policy rendezvous between Sashaying and Ralph, and this Volvo's job was merely to document the time and spot.

In fact, Ralph regarded these two or three behind him as not so much tails as escorts, their task to ensure his ideas for the future were not put at risk. Iles and Harpur would be aware that in Ralph Ember they had a gem, a bulwark, a stanchion. He tried to remember what Sashaying's woman was like, in case she needed some looking after if Vernon did go deep custodial. He could be described as reasonably presentable and with fair earnings, and so might have pulled something attractive and clean, possibly still clean, despite him. Perhaps his loony sort of glide-walk that got him called Sashaying appealed to certain women. You could never guess what would touch off a woman. Think of the hunchback of Notre Dame. He was deformed and short but never short of it. And then Charlie Chaplin.

Ralph parked. For the last half mile he had lost sight of the tails and he waited in his car a few minutes now for the Volvo to arrive or pass and give him a better view than in the mirror. But it must have turned off earlier. What did that mean? Had he been wrong to think they were tracking him? A bit of egomania? Or in the final part of the trip had they guessed where he must be going and pulled away to avoid notice when he stopped? Ralph locked his Saab and went into the restaurant. Sashaying was at the bar. Ember called for a gin and bitters. At least Sashaying didn't have

117

on that fucking take-cover siren suit he turned up in at the Monty on bail day.

'Ralph,' he cried, 'let's make of this spot for a couple of hours a centre of calm and wisdom in the current bewildering pattern of things.'

'Do your lawyers expect you to go down?' Ember replied.

'And let me say I'm grateful you can, as it were, put things on hold and fit me into your schedule, Ralph. I did not count on it. How could I count on it? You're getting all-way pressures, some enormous.'

'The thing about barristers is they have to talk optimism, not just to the client, but to themselves, so they keep buoyant, all-out in the fight. Like football coaches. They don't always let you see their true estimate of prospects.'

'Oh, yes, harsh pressures on you. I think of the tales that you knew about Stave Street in advance and gave a whisper to Harpur, so he could be there at the spot-on moment. People could see a plot there to wipe out all sorts, one way or the other. This is bound to give you tension, Ralph. Whisperers are always liable to get it bad. I don't say Curly was a whisperer, but we could both name others who came to serious grief. You were wise to bring the interesting kid home from France, but even so your worries won't just die, will they?'

'We were keen on a properly rounded pre-university education for my daughter – part France, part here. This was all schemed in her infancy. My wife is what could be called a long-term planner, as far as schooling for the children is concerned, Vernon.'

'And I could easily understand it, for instance, if you were getting bad doubts about Manse Shale, too,' Sashaying replied. 'You'd be loyal to him, I know. This is an enduring association. But others are asking whether he can adapt to what's happening, or is he stuck back there with his Pre-Raphaelites. Not that it's easy to adapt to what's happening, because I don't think any of us are sure in detail what *is* happening. But some will do better at adjustment than others. Clearly you – you, Ralph, are a strange

118

and brilliant mixture of the supremely constant and yet also the supremely flexible.'

'I take a steady look at things, at things however they might be – fixed or variable – and I try then to form a view,' Ember said. 'I think I can state this is what I'm known for. You hear people talk in their self-important ways about "business plans", "business projections" – well, this is the basis of *my* business plans, *my* business projections – an unhurried, careful examination of matters as they are at the moment of examination and then a judgement on which to base action. I don't claim any special distinction for this. My mother always used to say, "Think before you act, Ralph," and that's my watchword.'

'Manse Shale at the Agincourt session, looking very shaky and passé, I hear. Flip-charts – nearly as quaint and olde worlde as the mock medieval gear around the walls there – halberds and breastplates. To a considerable degree you have to carry him. This loads you, Ralph, bound to. And then that damn insult.'

'Which?' Ember asked.

'Iles.'

'What?'

'Disarming you in front of the people there, some very subordinate. This was certain to be bad for image. Like making a kid turn his pockets out when something's been nicked.'

'I don't see it that way,' Ember replied. This fucking cell potential was trying to break his legs and get him on the floor before the serious chat. Definitely a deal must be the idea.

'You're always forgiving, Ralph. Perhaps too much.'

'Do they say what sort of sentence, if you do go down?' Ember replied. 'You've got form, haven't you? So seven, eight?'

Sashaying was drinking a very pale sherry – what you could expect for someone wanting to seem civilized before getting clinked again. In a way, Ralph felt moved. He always pitied those forced to put on a social act. He did not quarrel with Sashaying's suit. Like Denzil's, it had probably been made for him and gave good room for his armpits to breathe. This would be important with his walking style because the effort must cause buckets of sweat. The suit's wool looked decent and it was respectably dark, but with an interesting fleck or two of something. His shoes were at least £175 and black. It hurt to think of all this stuff stuck away for years.

'Someone like Denzil Lake – will he sit tamely under a leader who's lost it?' Vernon asked.

'Denzil? He sits tamely behind a wheel. He's a fucking chauffeur,' Ember said.

'And?'

'Baggage man.'

'The thing with chauffeurs is they see plenty, hear plenty, about the business. Know-alls. Shale the democratic twat doesn't pull the Jaguar's partition window over.'

'Denzil? Denzil? You honestly think Denzil might try a coup?' Ember asked.

'Of course, he'd need to keep up the connection with you – your good offices. He'd realize he couldn't do things solo, not at first. It's why I wanted this get-together, Ralph.'

He knew why Sashaying wanted the sodding get-together. 'Which things couldn't he do solo?' Ember replied.

'Manse is not going to move aside willingly, is he?'

'Denzil will move him?'

'Bound to be a possible, Ralph.'

'Not something I've even thought about.'

'He's carrying weaponry now, I'm told,' Sashaying said.

'Who?'

'Denzil. Double weaponry, in fact. Iles made a show of that, didn't he – same as the humiliation he gave you?'

'I don't at all see it like that,' Ember replied.

Vernon said: 'I'd expect Denzil to make an approach.'

'To me?'

'But subtle. Roundabout, maybe. It could be dangerous,' Sashaying said. 'After all, Manse is a friend, isn't he, as well as a colleague? You might blow it all to him. Where would Denzil be then? Beaten to death with a flip-chart?'

'We're far into the hypothetical here,' Ember replied. 'I don't think Denzil would ever even try to start a move against Manse. Denzil looks a fright and talks horse shit, but he's foursquare for Shale.'

Sashaying Vern said: 'I was pleased to –'

'What happens to your operation if you do go down?' Ember asked. 'I'm afraid I forget your home situation. Dependants?'

'There's Maria, of course. Two kids.'

Christ, yes, Maria. She was not a beauty, or Ralph would have remembered her unprompted, but first rate tallness and verve. Verve could make up for all sorts. Sashaying had brought her to the Monty, possibly only once. She never handled Ember's scar, he felt almost certain of this, but her verve stuck with him. Verve was the only term. 'Preparations might be needed,' Ember said.

They went into the dining room. He ordered a goat's cheese starter, then cassoulet. Sashaying had tomato soup and a steak well done. That seemed about right for him. Sashaying was of a piece. You could say that for him – the walk, and the sherry and the standard issue steak. They drank Chablis and Pomerol, half bottles because of the driving. Luckily, Sashaying asked Ember to choose. Sashaying would probably not even know what cassoulet was until it arrived in the pot. Ralph observed extremely likeable girls at two of the tables with very ungifted men in dud garb, but saw nobody he knew. Of course, many customers might recognize him, though, through his position at the Monty. Now and then, he hated the whole young Chuck Heston thing, because it made people stare and perhaps get intrusive. Goat's cheese was probably something Charlton would not have gone for in a restaurant, thinking it lowly and peasant, and one reason Ralph picked it was to break himself out from the resemblance for a while. Goat's cheese furnished another factor in that Ember identity quest.

'Some call you Panicking Ralph, or even Panicking Ralphy, but not me, I assure you,' Sashaying said.

'Panicking Ralph? I have heard that. Yes, one hears it and laughs – it's such an absurd slander, built on envy.'

'I wouldn't be here now, would I, if I believed that kind of thing? And the fact Iles disarms you first at the Agincourt doesn't have to mean he considered you the feeblest and least likely to resist – Ralphy, the push-over.'

'Jazz musician, Lester Young, used to walk the way you do,' Ember replied. 'They discovered it was gout.'

'I should think Denzil has already come and had a word with you about Manse. Denz was up the club, wasn't he – just arrived, no prelims, and fuck protocol – what you'd expect from him? Someone mentioned that to me.'

'Advice, Vern: I don't know jails, but I think it would be wiser not to do all that hip-jigging when you're in the recreation yard.'

'Scenario, Ralph, as I see it, Denzil turns up and suggests it's time to get rid of Manse and you don't disagree – don't actually *agree* because of all that fine friendship and so on, but don't altogether piss on the idea, either, seeing, in that style of yours, chances for Ralph W. Ember. Denz looks like something easier to deal with than Manse, doesn't he?'

'An organization like yours, Vern – in some ways healthy, no question, but only emergent as yet . . . an organization like that depends *so* much on the headman. If the headman gets removed – death, jail, disablement – this kind of organization is frighteningly vulnerable and frail and liable to break-up. All right, you'll say seven years is only three if you behave in there, but three in our trade is like half a century in more usual games. Things are all the time on the move. They need a focus. If that focus is absent from a young firm for as much as three years, the structure will fall in on itself.'

'But then, say Manse is gone and you and Denz are hand-in-gloving, or seeming to, is Denz going to be satisfied with that for keeps? He'll want totality, won't he? You know it. Would you be able to cope with him in that mood and mode? As I've said, I don't go with those who see you as a panicking wreck, Ralphy, but –'

'You've picked your staff carefully, I'm sure of that, Vern, yet when they see the boss do something as fucking dim as traceable menaces so he's given a true thump by the court – then they'll start wondering about their future. Maria. Any of your jolly lads sniffing around there? This is a woman with . . . well, with a lot of verve, as I recall her. You're wonderfully fortunate. Yes, verve is the word for Maria. You, removed for three, four years minimum.'

'So, what I'm proposing, Ralph – well, you can see it, I know – you've got that sort of marvellous, intuitive brain. That's how I'd prefer to regard you, not as someone always liable to free-fall into panic. We let Denz do the job on Shale. Why not? And then once Denz is up there, installed, thinking he's great and safe, some of my best people take him definitively out. This would eliminate a filthy threat to you, Ralph, without any kind of connection for Harpur and Iles to work on. Anon entirely. Like *Strangers on a Train*. No obvious motives. And there'd be an agreement between you and me that when Denz is gone my outfit and yours co-exist and mutually profit, the way yours and Manse's do now. Because I esteem you, Ralph, I'd be prepared to take your word on this. A handshake, nothing else.'

'The whole secret in cassoulet is the way the beans are soaked,' Ember replied. 'This is a dish you can't rush. It's from the south-west part of France.'

'Plus, as well as Denz, we'd be willing to look after anything rough towards you coming out of the Stave Street situation.'

Ember chuckled and said: 'I don't think I need the –'

'It's obvious Denzil would have to go at some stage. What I hear is, when he was up the club some magic seemed to get pulsing between him and Venetia. She's quite an active kid for her age, I gather. Well, why else did you whoosh her to France? This is a kid who's not afraid of the older man, even an older man like Denz. All right, she'd be damned upset if he became a loss, but it would be for her ultimate advantage.'

'I'd say about seventy per cent chance you'll go down,' Ember replied.

'You've been talking to Rosie QC, have you?'

'She says seventy?'

'Seventy or seventy-five. About that,' Sashaying said. 'I'm paying them treasure, but they don't think they can do it. Why I need you, Ralph. Why I see my position's frail and I can't ask for more than a handshake. If I'm inside we'd communicate through Maria, naturally. She'd visit and bring me your account of things, and I'd reply. I know you've got a hell of a timetable, what with the club, the business and letters to the Press, but maybe you could fit her in for a face-to-face just now and then. It couldn't be phones or letters or e-mail.' He giggled, steak in his mouth a bit too much on view. 'God, listen to me talking to Ralph Ember about basic security. I'm an idiot. It's the brilliant wines.'

'Pomerol – the Merlot grape,' Ralph replied. 'Gentle, warm, confiding. Face-to-face would be essential.'

Ember had parked at a main street meter outside the restaurant, hoping the red Volvo would pass him there so he could get a proper look at the occupants. Sashaying's car was in a side road fifty yards away. It would be habit with him, and with Ember usually, to put his vehicle where it might not be noticed by patrols – anyone's patrols. They left each other at the door of the Grenoble. The handshake Vern had spoken of took place, Vern prolonging it, his face intent and comradely under the Grenoble's porch light. Ralph did not mind this handshake. After all, it hardly amounted to a handshake at all, as Ralph thought of handshakes, since it referred to so much that was only talk, hope, speculation. How could a handshake based on ifs signify? If . . . if . . . if the ifs materialized, the time might come to give Sashaying true thought, wherever he might be. Perhaps a handshake would be impossible then, but Ralph was sure he could fix his timetable to make room for Maria instead now and then. 'I'm sorry if occasionally

I seemed to lose attention, Ralph,' Sashaying said, 'but I was getting big come-on looks from one of those fannies in there.'

'Oh?'

'Yes.'

'Which?'

Sashaying described the more sexy of the two women Ralph had noticed in the restaurant. It enraged him to hear Sashaying claim for himself signals unquestionably aimed at Ralph. Also, he deplored the gross term Vernon used for women. Ember loathed anything that seemed to reduce other human beings, whether or not women. Respect could be given to women, even if they paired themselves with slobs for the sake of a dinner, as those two did.

In his Saab, Ralph watched for the Volvo in case it had lurked, but could not see it, not at once. He switched on the lights and engine and was about to pull out when he heard what sounded to him through the car glass like gunshots, seven, possibly eight, rapid gunshots. Almost immediately afterwards, the Volvo appeared at the corner of the side street where Vern had gone for his car. It entered the main drag and went away fast in the opposite direction from where Ralph was parked. He kept the engine running and the lights on but stayed there, staring at the junction. What came to him instantly was a stupendous and familiar compulsion to do a bunk. One of his panics began. A line of sweat formed across his shoulder blades and began to drip down his back and collect on the elastic waistband of his underpants, an icy patch. His eyes lost focus so that for a couple of seconds he couldn't make out clearly any longer the side street corner. He thought people moved about there, though. He rubbed his eyes with the backs of his hands to try to get them right again and this worked not too badly, except sweat from his skin caused stinging. Yes, three or four people were grouped at the junction and seemed hesitant about entering the side street. Perhaps others had already gone.

He thought his legs would be all right – that is, all right to work the car pedals and get him a good fucking distance from here. Ember had a marvellous flair for putting miles between himself and bad perils, as Venetia would call them. By bad he meant perils which were perils only, with no possible plus aspects for him. Panic brought cloud to some areas of his mind but gave a special, traditional clarity to other sections. These told him it would be foolhardy to get closer to whatever had just happened. Of course, he had a notion what had happened. He did not need his mind at full operation for that. Sashaying had been ambushed. He was most likely dead or hurt in or near his car. But ambushed from an unmarked police vehicle? That notion shook both bits of Ralph's mind. Had they followed Ember so as to pinpoint Vernon? But how would they know Ralph had been on his way to meet him? Why target Vern? Had the planned target been Vern only? Was Ralph lucky to be parked somewhere else? Would it be barmy to place himself nearer to whatever remained of Sashaying?

Ralph abandoned the questions. What he saw as certainty was the massive hazard of involvement in this slippery sequence. Or, at least, further involvement. It was going to come out, wasn't it, that he had dined with Sashaying at the Grenoble? There would have to be some kind of investigation, even if this were a police execution, one of Iles's little ploys. Despite the egomaniac suggestion from Sashaying, both those two attractive girls in the restaurant had probably spent most of their time eyeing Ralph, and he did not blame them, when you thought what they were sitting with. But it would mean they could give a description. He did sometimes regret his famed profile and the fascination his jaw scar produced in women. They seemed to think that because the mark had once been a wound, they could find a way into him there, and if allowed real closeness would start fingering it.

As a matter of fact, in one of his major panics, such as now, Ember himself always feared the scar would open up. He imagined something foul and intimate dripping down his front. Absurd, obviously. He put up a couple of fingers to check, though, and felt slightly calmed to find it dry.

Those women in the Grenoble could even have known who he was. The one Sashaying mentioned had, in fact, offered several small smiles when Ralph gave her some sympathetic stare, which might indicate only aching excitement but could also mean recognition. The management of the Grenoble definitely would be aware who he was, although Vern booked the table.

However, dining with him was so different from being caught alongside the body, if that's what he was now, a body – caught either by the Volvo on a re-prowl, or by the emergency troupe who would answer 999 calls soon. In any case, although Ember knew he had enough power in his legs to work the car pedals, he doubted they were capable of a walk to the scene. He could drive the little distance, perhaps, but the Saab would certainly identify him. As he saw it, the most mature response for him must be absence. Frequently, absence had been one of Ember's prime strengths, as say prayer was to a priest and ripeness to a peach.

All right, Harpur or someone else would be around the club eventually to ask about the Grenoble dinner, but Ralph could take eventually. It was the nowness of now that troubled him – the possibility of bullets or of getting suspect-listed. If they'd wanted to do Sashaying plus Ember, they might decide to frame him, as a fall-back. *Eventually*, he could say he had certainly enjoyed a business dinner with Sashaying, but that they had parted at the restaurant door and Ralph knew nothing of him until Vern and those shots hit the media. Of course, it might have been officers acting for Iles who did the ambush, and this could ensure inquiries were only formal. They'd make the Volvo disappear at a breaker's or a lake.

Fuck it, no. No. NO. He could not do a runner. Contemptible to think of it. Ralph turned on himself, despised himself. It was all to do with that identity matter, wasn't it? In the Grenoble, when Ember had been feeling at his assured best because of the polished choice of goat's cheese, cassoulet and the wines, Sashaying suddenly came in with that talk about 'Panicking Ralph'. The aim was to

127

shake Ember, of course, and get Sashaying into dominance, a cheap, brutal trick, and one Ralph had often experienced from others. But, if he galloped off, it would be an admission that Vern had things right, and the panicking side of Panicking was the real, ruling one. And in a way it might, in fact, be the right one. Ralph did have panics. He was panicking now. But panic itself might not be contemptible. Anyone could panic. Doctors and counsellors recognized a syndrome called 'panic attacks' and tried to treat them. They were like an illness. No, it was the caving in to panic and an abject dash for safety that showed a man to be yellow on yellow.

Ember must avoid that. Must. He was Ralph W. Ember, not Panicking Ralph or Ralphy. He switched off the Saab and opened the driver's door. He swung his legs out, really swung them, a bold, virtually debonair move, the kind of athleticism that would be natural for Ben Hur. Ember recognized obligations to himself and to his image. He got his feet down with true firmness on the pavement and sensed – almost knew – but at least sensed, that when he brought the rest of him out of the car and tried to stand his legs would work and bear him triumphantly. Upright was his natural position, not cowering and sweating and caressing his scar. Likewise he thought walking feasible now. Part of his mind might still be paralysed by dread, but another part had a clear grasp of what walking amounted to – knew it entailed putting one foot in front of the other and repeating that to achieve progress.

He banged the Saab door behind him with the same kind of flourish as when bringing his legs out. This decisive slamming showed he could put himself outside the security of the car cabin and meet things direct. He applied the locks, then started off down the road towards the side street on the right. Gravity and movement caused some of that sweat pool at the base of Ember's back to get inside the waistband of his underpants and run down his buttocks and legs. This he ignored. He could not be deterred. He had set his mind on that fifty yard walk, and his will would help him crack it.

He viewed the wreckage of Sashaying's face without almost any satisfaction at all, despite the rampant way Vern had boasted of the woman's supposed fascination with his looks. Nobody deserved this degree of ruin, regardless of vanity. They had caught him just as he was about to enter his car. Only his head, face and top of his chest must have been available above the car roof to the gun, or guns, as the Volvo came down the street, perhaps pausing for a second to make sure the barrage worked. It did. Ember thought the weapon or weapons must have been large calibre. It was short range but, even so, the damage seemed big. He had fallen down into the gutter alongside his old Mondeo, twisting his body as he went so he finished on his back. Perhaps he had been fighting to stay standing, scrabbling at the car for support. A wide line of blood started on the roof of the Mondeo and splotched the window and driver's door.

A small crowd of passers-by stood around Vern. A woman wept. Another yelled for help into a mobile phone. 'Turf war, most likely,' a man said.

'My God, it's like Manchester,' the weeping woman said.

'Shot, yes, shot in – what's the name of this fucking street, Al?' the woman with the mobile asked.

'Talisman,' the man who had spoken of a turf war said.

'Dead? He looks dead,' the woman told the mobile. 'But send an ambulance as well as the heavies.'

'The streets were quiet and safe for years, the pushing beautifully contained, but now suddenly this, because of changes,' Al said. 'I'd call it tragic. No apologies for that.'

'No, nobody's touched him,' the woman with the mobile said. 'Not enough of his mouth left to try kiss of life.'

'Although probably only a small-timer, he gets this,' Al said. 'Look at the car. Next stop scrap. But good shoes.'

Ralph bent over Vern, truly close. It seemed necessary – some sort of commiseration. 'Do you know him at all?' the weeping woman asked.

'Turf war?' Ralph replied. He stood up again. 'What's that? Race course gangs?'

'Drugs,' Al said. 'Disputed territory. Often in the Press.'

'But that's awful,' Ralph replied. To crouch with Sashaying briefly had been so right. It was a comradeship gesture, a manly gesture, the reverse of panic. After all, this had been a dinner companion and almost a business colleague. It would be harsh to think of Sashaying only as someone who did pale sherry for effect. He did do pale sherry for effect, but to Ralph this was understandable. Vern had wanted to appear sophisticated and eligible as a possible trade associate, even when in jug. The prospect of jail often made men anxious about funds. Households were held together by funds. Verve alone would not do it for Maria. Sashaying wanted her to be still at home when he came out, thought Ralph might be able to help with that.

And so, Sashaying had felt he must impress him. Vern was at the earliest stages of a commercial vocation and Ember would seem titanic. Ralph often received such reverence from novices. He did not despise it. He considered that to lower himself physically in the street like that as an act of sympathy with Sashaying's body and face – above all, his face – was a decent gesture and typically humane. Sashaying had obviously prized his body and face. Ralph wondered about possibly going back to the restaurant in case he could get a quick, private word in the vestibule with the prettier of those two girls while her man fetched the car or had a pee. Ralph might be able to slip her a business card with his number on it. He would not mention the blasting of Vern because it couldn't interest her and might darken an otherwise positive chat. Most probably she would not remember Sashaying at all, except as someone of no significance, unfamiliar with class menus, who happened to have been with Ralph.

The mobile phone woman had finished talking to Emergency Services. She said: 'He passed us on foot in the main street. I noticed the way he walked. Like a glide?'

'That right?' Ember replied.

'Kind of sashaying, you know.'

'A word I haven't heard for an age,' Ember said. 'Always, it makes me think of the Deep South and its relaxed style.'

'We actually remarked on the walk.'

'I expect he'll have some identification on him,' Ember said. 'But we must leave it for the police.'

'That walk – I wondered whether a spat between gays,' she replied.

'Some spat,' Al said.

'They can be vicious and dreadfully competitive,' she said.

'An open mind is best,' Ember replied.

'The old banger car,' she said, 'well, you mentioned it yourself, Al, it's not right for drugs. Usually this year's top of the range BMW.'

'The shoes. Brilliant,' Al said.

'But shoes are minor,' she replied.

'Show me a man's shoes and I'll tell you his bank balance,' Al said.

'Arsehole,' she replied. 'You're pissed.'

On the way back to his car, Ralph did call in at the Grenoble and told the waiter he might have left some keys on the table. 'Some kind of disturbance out there?' the waiter asked. 'It sounded like shots.'

'Honestly?'

The waiter said the table had been cleared and nothing found but took Ralph back to it. The prettier woman and her man were still liqueuring. She looked over and gave Ralph a real glance – no question the kind of glance Sashaying would never get, and had never got tonight, the arrogant, dead jerk. Ralph felt this glance to be a genuine glance, only helped along, not *created*, by cognac. Because she was evidently intrigued, Ralph explained: 'Some keys – thought I might have left some keys.'

'Oh, I didn't notice any,' she replied. The voice was good. Concerned. Warm. He was used to that kind of warmth when women spoke to him. She stood up and came over to the table. The man stayed where he was and looked indifferent.

131

'I've been through all my pockets,' Ralph said. He pantomimed another search with both hands. His right found a few business cards in his jacket pocket. His left found the keys in his trousers pocket, where they had always been and where he knew they were. He produced them and did some shamefacedness for quite a while. 'Damn. What a fool! Here they are. Sorry. Forgive the fuss. But thanks for your concern.' He put out his right hand to shake hers in gratitude and she smiled and did not show she had taken the card. If you were lying ruined at feet level against a very faded car you were not going to be able to pull a piece of brilliance like this. Ralph certainly did not regard it as harsh to wonder whether this woman had done similar manoeuvres before.

'We thought shots in the street,' she said.

'I hope not, sincerely.'

He had Bart Haverson's address and drove over there now. One of the great features of his present commercial position was the noting of talented folk and bringing them on, as a soccer coach or drama teacher might spot tomorrow's stars. It was a kind of investment – one based on some judgement by Ralph, but also on what he saw as a near-magical element of intuition. He valued intuition. Obviously, he valued judgement as well, but he thought there would always be a place for the gifted hunch.

This explained his interest in Bart and Delphine. To Ralph's clairvoyant eye they gleamed promise. Probably what Sashaying lacked was the guidance of hunch, or he might have realized that a dark side street for parking did not suit this time, though often fine. It must have been part hunch that kept Ralph on the main road. But, of course, any man who could so idiotically fail to see a woman felt fascinated not by him but by Ralph was not going to have good hunches, or even good judgement. If that bird did ring and even mentioned Sashaying he would put the fucking phone down and unplug.

Luckily, Bart Haverson's mother lived with him and his girlfriend, so Ember could put a proposal to Bart and Delphine at once. They had a big detached place up near

132

Iles's house with the dopey name, Idylls, at Rougemont Place. Ralph always thought suburbia OK. People had to live somewhere and few could afford a property and grounds like his Low Pastures, though the Haversons' house would cost. Perhaps Mrs Haverson had money behind her from somewhere. Folk in these kinds of houses often stacked in building societies or gilts. Romona, the girlfriend, was excluded from their discussions and Ember regretted this – regarded it as cold and hurtful. But Bart said she preferred not to know anything about the trade and would decline to attend a meeting even if invited. Ember still felt it damned unmannerly to go off with the other two into a closed room, but Romona was a bit of a lump with grim dress sense.

'As I see it,' Ember said, 'now the commerce has been given a kind of unofficial but real approval, we'll need to extend the firm's higher level posts. Clearly, selling is still the main task and I'm here tonight to ask you, Bart, to assume the duties of chief sales executive. This isn't a position we've ever needed to define in the past. Beau Derek, in fact, handled it until his death, but never with the title actually used. My feeling is we cannot continue in this casual way, given the increased status of trafficking.'

'Wow! – a shock, Ralph, but a pleasant one, of course,' Bart replied. 'I hope I'll –'

'You can undoubtedly handle it,' Ember said. To look after people's confidence was a crux leadership role.

'Of course you can, Bart!' his mother cried. 'Congratulations, darling.'

The decoration of this house seemed to Ember quite fair. There was reasonably civilized wallpaper, none of that fucking red flock stuff you could sometimes get when an older woman had money, and no straight-up-and-down black and white so-called Regency stripes, either. This room they were in had a nice floral pattern to the paper, the colours pretty well believable. The furniture was brown leather, with brass studs, a traditional style dating right back, maybe to Attlee. Someone kept the cushions very well plumped up and Ralph felt glad these people

133

could have their little comforts. They drank coffee. Ember said: 'And then I sense the need for certain ancillary yet vital departments in the firm now. I believe you can help us with this, Delphine.'

'Ancillary?' she said.

'I have in mind a public relations section,' Ember replied. 'I see you as an admirable head of that.'

'Well, it *sounds* wonderful,' she said, 'but what does a public relations section do?'

'It relates, ma,' Bart answered. 'It relates the firm to the public.'

Delphine said: 'Yes, but –'

'The days when secrecy and furtiveness were the essence of trading are probably over,' Ember replied. 'Firms like mine will be concerned how to establish what some would call their "image" with the customers. I would prefer the word "character" or even "personality" – in the way, for instance, Fortnum and Mason's name instantly suggests a particular and special kind of store, or Cadbury's chocolate has a distinctive presence and reputation.'

'We can't label our coke packets "By Appointment to Her Majesty the Queen",' Bart said. He had a laugh about this for a while. Ralph let him. Humour could be all right now and then. Often Ralph was tolerant of jokes and wit, even from subordinates.

'When there are unpleasantnesses in the street, I need someone who can deal with the media and put our point of view effectively,' Ralph said. 'A single, capable voice with an agreed statement, like New Labour's demand that its people get "on message". Your work has two aspects. First, you initiate good material about the firm to the media or direct to the public – our abhorrence of violence, my interest in many environmental topics, frequently expressed through letters to the Press. Second, you will be ready to react when some incident or event seems to endanger our reputation.'

'This sounds an interesting and forward-looking role,' Delphine replied.

'There! You're already talking like a public relations executive, ma,' Bart said.

'The firms are not totally legit, obviously,' Ralph said. 'This tolerance we get is only partial and unspoken. It's when an organization is in that kind of shadowy area that it most needs sensitive public relations. Think of Nixon. For instance, talking of the need to be prepared with a reaction, Sashaying Vernon was shot tonight and –'

'Oh, my God,' Delphine cried. 'Where? How?' Her body had stiffened and her voice shook.

'This is terrible,' Bart said. He stood from one of the studded armchairs and went to kneel alongside his mother, who was in another.

Ember said: 'It's bad, yes, but not by any means –'

'Mother had a relationship with Vernon a couple of years ago.'

'Women find him – found him – enormously attractive,' she said.

'You fucking what?' Ember replied.

'Was it a jealousy thing – the killing?' she asked. 'Poor Vernon. I was older than he, of course, but . . . and there were others even while he and I –'

'It might be a police execution,' Ember said. 'His face was carefully destroyed. Their kind of high-spirited jape.'

'Oh, God, God,' Delphine gasped.

'Utterly,' Ember said. 'I don't want to talk much about this. It's not seemly. But destroyed. Utterly. His face.'

'Police?' Bart said. 'You're certain?'

'You doubt they're capable of it?' Ember replied.

Bart said: 'Not if you –'

'Some maverick group within the Force,' Ember said.

'Well, yes, feasible,' Bart said.

'Very professional tailing,' Ember said. 'They were behind me first.'

'Do you mean they wanted you as well?' Bart asked.

'I'm a bit wily for that kind of treatment.'

'But not Vern?' Bart said.

'He had things to learn, so many,' Ember replied.

135

'But why would the police want to do him?' Bart asked.

'That's why I'm suggesting a public relations department,' Ember said. 'We need to have a worked-out response when the media hear of it and start asking around. Of course, the fucking police will have *their* Press department issuing a version that suits Iles's purpose in getting Vern slaughtered – whatever it is. We must be able to match this – yes, like that rebuttal machinery Mandelson created for Tony Blair at Labour HQ.'

'Iles?' Bart replied. 'I thought the new Chief had his own ideas.'

'Iles,' Ralph replied.

'In any public place – a pub, restaurant, party – women noticed Vern,' Delphine said. 'I mean, *noticed* him.' Bart stood, squeezed her shoulder, then went back to his own chair.

'My plan, Delph, when the Press and TV people come looking for a comment or an insight on Sashaying dead is I refer them to you and you say no connection with us, minnows squabbling. The aim is to show that, even in the chaos conditions brought on by unofficial legalizing, some firms, like ours, retain that dignity and restraint which gives them, in fact, a virtually normal, proper business status. What upstart, grasping outfits like Sashaying's do is entirely different – marginal to the central scene. These will be private, unofficial briefings you give, obviously no TV appearances! You will be an immense plus – a well-spoken, modest, mature lady. I think you should aim for a sadness in your tone. Make sadness the motif. This would arise from regret that one or two minor figures in the commercial context might bring taint on established firms – the dead man in this case being due to appear in court on very serious charges.'

'He could be hasty,' Delphine Haverson said. 'I admit he could be hasty.'

'It would be unwise for you to attend the funeral,' Ember replied. 'Our whole object must be to put big space between him and us. An anon wreath would certainly be all right. If you did delphiniums and signed it Trixie V. Williamson or Patience Cartwright "with deep regrets" that would get your feelings over, wouldn't it? Nobody wants to belittle those, believe me.'

Ember called in at the Monty to see the manager had things running all right, then just before midnight went home to Low Pastures. Margaret was still up watching a video of *Fargo* where the woman cop and her husband eat so much. He poured a couple of armagnacs and sat with her. Social events such as the contacts with Sashaying and the Haversons were not the kinds of meetings Ember would mention to Margaret. He considered her a wonderful, precious person and, obviously, mother of his daughters, but she did not understand the commercial side of things properly. Or not *all* the commercial side. She was certainly good with the Monty – its accounts, staff arrangements, ordering of stock – but she didn't always recognize the full importance of the trade in substances. Ralph would not compare her with Bart's Romona, who refused to hear about it and so could kid herself it did not exist. Margaret knew it was there, even knew it provided far and away the biggest part of their income, but she did not like it and wanted Ralph to go totally legal. She used to keep on about this more than she did now, but he saw the wish lingered and, in fact, he admired her for it, loved her extra for it. This was a woman with true values, unshakeable values. Ralph definitely did not treat her as half-baked for refusing to accept how crucial the trade was to them. No, simply, she saw the situation from a different point. Ralph respected her for this but plainly could not allow her attitude to fuck him about. That is, to fuck him about re this particular topic. On other aspects of their life he would quite often listen to her, even gladly listen to her sometimes.

To talk about a meal with Sashaying or the visit to the Haversons would upset Margaret because these get-togethers could mean only that Ralph was committed to expanding the commodities section. Although Margaret unquestionably possessed a quite developed mind, she

137

seemed to have trouble with that most elementary business precept – move forward or perish. If the original Marks and Spencer had not extended their sales methods beyond the market hand-carts they started with, who would have heard of them today? Margaret failed to appreciate that if Ember wanted to transform the Monty into a kind of Athenaeum or Garrick, considerable funds would be needed for constructing, say, a library and reading room, and for keeping the club alive while a new sort of membership was built. For now he needed the trade so as eventually to achieve what Margaret wanted – complete respectability. This idea seemed too tricky for her.

'I wonder if it would be an idea to keep the children home from school for a few days,' he said.

'What, after all the diplomacy and smarminess needed to get Venetia back in?' Margaret said.

'Only a few days.'

'Has something happened?' she asked.

The impossibility of talking to Margaret about the Grenoble dinner meant, inevitably, that Ralph could not tell her about Sashaying's blundering tumble into death. This would make the media tomorrow but Ralph knew it would be an error to refer to it now, on his return from the Haversons'. News of such a misfortune would probably make Margaret even less comfortable with the trade, and Ember's closeness to the incident was sure to fret her. Ralph would like to save her from stress. Maybe Margaret could learn some poise from Venetia – that way her hand must have felt the Beretta under his coat on the way to Corton, but no mention of it ever. 'It's just that I have a feeling,' he replied. 'Things are tensing up.'

'What things? What do you mean, for God's sake, "tensing up"?'

'We could say Ven and Fay have caught something from each other. Flu.'

'What's happened, Ralph?' She had begun to shout, but it was late and the girls should be asleep.

'This feeling – that things are tensing up. I've always believed in intuition, you know.'

138

Chapter Eight

Iles said: 'Someone like Sashaying hit that way – it's inexplicable. A fucking nobody, Col.'

'Francis Garland is on it for me,' Harpur replied. 'Of course, he says there's a buzz you set it up.'

'Yes, I heard.'

'To boost your chaos theory – get folk nostalgic for days when you had charge of everything, not the Chief. Next to no street violence. The holy alliance with Ralph and Manse.'

'Yes, I heard,' Iles said. 'Ever come across the word "concordat", Harpur?'

'The Volvo was stolen three days ago and found burned out at Cotter's Mound,' Harpur replied.

'Yes, I heard. What's the "of course" bit, you ponce?'

'How do you mean, sir – "What's the 'of course' bit?"'

'You said, "Of course, he says there's a buzz you set it up." What's the "of course" bit?'

'Garland's got people asking around the area and we gather from the Grenoble management that Ember was with Vern until five minutes before,' Harpur replied.

'Ralph's known.'

'Dinner with Sashaying. Oh, God, imagine it, Col – sitting opposite someone like that when he's feeding. I'm sad for Ralphy.' Iles did a period of sighing. 'But why should I say this? He's only like all the rest of us, confused, threatened by the new climate. What would a giant of Ember's experience be doing with a nail-paring like Vern?'

139

'Would you be able to organize this sort of thing, sir?' Harpur said.

'Which?'

'The ambush. Vern's facelift.'

'How do you mean, "organize", Col?'

'Obviously, you'd have the trickiness and natural brutality to put the scheme together. But finding the people. Three, we think, in the Volvo. When I say "organize" – well, could you find three of our officers who'd agree to something like that, even for you?'

'You're right, Col. Some officers do insist on an almost mystical loyalty to one's self. It can be an embarrassment. I tell them I'm not the only senior figure at headquarters who rates.'

'Is that right, sir?'

'Which?' Iles replied.

'Which what?'

'Is it right I *tell* them I'm not the only senior figure who rates? Or is it right I'm *not* the only senior figure who rates?'

'These are certainly problems worth looking at in a leisure period, sir.'

'Don't tell me, Harpur, that it would be permissible for Desmond Iles to have his little private group of retainers within our larger body,' Iles said. 'My own Praetorian Guard. But the last thing I see myself as, Col, is an emperor.'

'Is that right, sir?'

'I'm an Assistant Chief. Assistant. Assistant.' Iles loathed this title and found it a slur. He spoke now with all the s sounds given their full packet of sliminess and subordination.

'How would you instruct your Volvo party, sir? "Oh, what I'd like you to do, team, is locate Sashaying and waste his face as an extra to death. He's a sport and would understand, don't worry."'

'It's a good term, Col.'

'Which?'

'Organize.'

140

'Thanks.'

'As things slip further into the hell-hole after this lunacy from the top the importance of organizing against them grows. Indeed, *duty.*'

'Which "them", sir?'

'Things.'

'Seven shots, we believe, from a 9 mm Walther. Four hits. Only one gun firing. So why a crew of three? A driver, a marksman, and the other?'

'This does sound like a very nice degree of planning, Col. Even a reserve. Field Marshal Montgomery always demanded more troops than were necessary – a force fifteen to one bigger than the enemy's, Hemingway said. Malice.'

'Was the third one holding her/his ammo in case they found Ralph? As our stuff is almost all Heckler and Koch these days, the Walther's clever. Clever on a fairly primitive, obvious level, that is. Did you decide on the Walther, sir?'

'Or think how slack it was for Ember to agree to the Grenoble,' Iles replied. 'This is fucking flamboyance, Col. This is casualness. Was Ralphy ever like that? Would sloppiness bring him Low Pastures and the club? What's happened to discretion, security? That's why I say chaos, Harpur.'

'But *how* did you hear?'

'What?'

'The buzz.'

'Which?' Iles asked.

'That you sent the Volvo – field marshalled it all, like Montgomery.'

'It's a buzz. Around,' Iles replied. 'Unfair.'

'Is it?'

'Unkind.'

'But specifically,' Harpur said.

'Specifically what?'

'Who fucking told you.'

'It's the buzz.'

'Yes, but someone has to buzz it.'

141

'You know, you sound surprisingly damn capable when you're into interrogation-suite mode, Col. A face and breath like yours would help, shoving them at a poor stifled prat.'

'I think of you as a leader who loves transparency above all, sir,' Harpur replied.

'Thanks, Col. A buzz of that sort might begin with someone like Garland – or like Ralphy.'

'Garland?'

'Resentment. Revenge.'

'Ralphy or someone *like* Ralphy? Who's like Ralphy?'

'He's interested in me, my aims,' Iles said.

'You had the buzz from Ralphy?'

'I said he might have started it. Or Garland. Ralph's convinced I have what's called, in the jargon, "my own agenda".'

'Which agenda would that be?'

'You've put Francis Garland on it, have you?' Iles replied. His voice cantered towards hysteria.

'He has the experience, sir.'

'Oh, yes, he'd like to get me, you know. He had something going with Sarah. You're not the only one who's been there. He resents me still for pulling her away. Yet you give him the job. You *want* him to get me?'

'He'll do things with total impartiality, sir. Would that be OK?'

They were in Harpur's room at headquarters. Iles began to kick the bottom drawer of a metal filing cabinet in the harsh, thoughtful style he'd sometimes go in for when the topic was his wife. 'You trying to fit me up, Harpur? You're still after Sarah, too? What about your undergrad bed-mate? You want me gone – flung out of the job, jailed for Vern?' Iles had begun to scream. His voice would carry through the walls and closed door, but people were used to the ACC and did not let his fits interfere with their work or tea breaks. 'She laughs about you, she laughs about Garland, when occasionally of an evening after TV or reading *The Small House at Allington* to each other we look together at the past. You particularly she finds now –'

142

'To put three of our people in a car for this kind of job would be a daunting risk,' Harpur said, 'even for someone as shit-or-bust as you, sir. The possibility of fallings-out among them and subsequent leaks.'

'In some ways I see Ember's focus on me as touching, Col. It springs from a good, fruitful past. I'm one for tradition, the guarding of institutions.' He started to tremble slightly and now his voice took on a touch of emotional phlegminess. 'For instance, marriage I see as an institution that should be –'

'At least one of the three would have to be smart on car theft. Perhaps that explains the extra crew member.'

'He had a girlfriend, didn't he?' Iles replied.

'Who?'

'Sash.'

'Maria. A lot of verve.'

'Yes, I'd heard that,' Iles said.

'How?'

'The buzz. Verve was the word that came over often about her in the buzz.'

Iles wanted to see the spot where Sashaying got it. Again that resemblance to the old Chief. First there had been the Iles visit to Curly's burned place, now this. Yes, an imitation of Mark Lane's need to turn up at the site of any crime he considered symbolic – that is, symbolic of the final, oncoming catastrophic breakdown in system and order he feared. Lane would give such spots immeasurable grief and take a dreadful hammering from self-blame. Or possibly Iles needed a look at the pay-off point to his project.

Harpur had been called there during the night, of course, when Sashaying was found. He drove Iles now. The Mondeo remained in place, still with the broad blood drag marks. It and an area around had been taped off. Two pairs of detectives with clipboards door-knocked. Five or six more officers in dungarees and gloves searched front gardens. A police caravan stood parked halfway down the street as Francis Garland's Incident Room. Harpur and Iles went in and stood listening. Garland was talking to a

143

middle-aged man and woman, all of them seated on wooden folding chairs.

'Myself, I thought gunfire,' the woman said, 'but Al decided, at that juncture, probably fireworks. You said kids fooling, probably fireworks, didn't you, Al?'

'It being usually best not to jump to a dramatic interpretation of something like that,' Al said. 'We're out on the main street, people all around. You don't expect shooting, do you? I mean, where's normality?'

'So true,' Iles said. 'Normality has ceased to be normal and in the future will cease to be normal even more.'

'But then the Volvo appears and belts off and I thought, Hello,' Al replied. 'If I could have got a paper and pencil out I'd have taken the number. By then I knew it was something. The way they accelerated. A 7 and a W in the reg. I can't do better than that, I'm afraid. And Madge also had the W and maybe a double 7. But I expect if you put a 7 or possibly a double 7 and a W into the computer with red Volvo you'll get a shortish list out you can check, especially if it's double 7.'

'We have the car,' Garland said.

'Oh?' Al replied.

'Just the car,' Garland said.

'Torched?' Al said.

'Well, obviously, we didn't rush into this street,' Madge said. 'It was darkish and very quiet by then. In that kind of situation, no knowing. There could have been others. His strange walk, like on skates – we wondered what we were dealing with.' She stood up and did a few gliding steps back and forth in the caravan. Garland watched and nodded and she sat down again. 'This walk didn't bring viewers of it calm. There were other people. Several said about that walk. Nervousness. For a bit we stood on the corner looking down the street. I thought someone in the gutter by the Mondeo but Al wasn't sure, were you, Al? He suggested a shadow or possibly a black plastic rubbish bag.'

'Sometimes, in the past, a bag outside someone's house like that in the dark – I've thought maybe a drunk asleep or even a road casualty. So I'm cautious now. I ponder pre any action. I've got to admit, there was a certain bulk that made me think not a bag of rubbish, but I kept options open at that stage.'

'I had the mobile and I said to Al, "Do I do 999?"'

'Well, I decided at the stage, premature,' Al said. 'We could come out of it looking alarmist – wasting police time.'

'What about Volvo occupants?' Garland asked.

'What?' Al replied.

'How many? Description,' Garland said.

'Two in the front, one possibly female – the driver, but a baseball cap pulled right down, track suit top – hard to be certain. One, maybe two, in the back. Gender? Not sure of those,' Al said.

'They didn't seem right for a Volvo,' Madge said.

'Oh, that's crazy, Madge,' Al replied. 'Builders, circus folk, snooker pros – all sorts these days have Volvos. You're tied up with what's referred to as image. For you, Volvo equals chartered surveyor.'

'Young, except for the front passenger,' Madge said.

'Yes, perhaps quite young,' Al said, 'but some young will drive a Volvo because they want the social clout or, if an estate, for the space to carry second-hand furniture when they've just got a house or flat.'

'And the front passenger, sort of crude-looking,' Madge said. 'I couldn't say anything about the others, but, yes, the front passenger looked crude.'

'In what way?' Garland asked.

'Unkempt. Thuggish,' she replied.

'I don't go along with that,' Al said. 'We heard a terrible, stupid rumour they could be police.'

'If they were police they could have made themselves look unkempt and thuggish, as disguise,' Madge said. 'This is well known among police.'

'There was even a name in the rumours,' Al said. His voice fell, as if extra secrecy were needed.

'A name of someone in the car?' Garland asked.

'A name of who scenarioed it all,' Al replied.

145

'This is an Assistant Chief Constable,' Madge said.
'Iles?' Garland asked.
'So, do you have to put the name in her fucking mouth, you trite louse?' Iles said.
'Yes, Assistant Chief Constable Desmond Iles,' Madge said. 'Rumour only.'
'We'd stress this,' Al said.
Madge turned and looked at Iles. 'Is that you, then?'
'Do you know this man?' Iles replied. 'I mean, really know him.'
'Which?'
'The thin-lipped pretty boy interviewing you,' Iles said. 'Al's got it written down, haven't you, Al?'
Al read from a piece of paper: 'Chief Inspector Francis –'
Iles said: 'This is a man who, regardless of decency, loyalty, honour, inveigled himself into –'
'How about their clothes?' Harpur said.
'Whose?' Al asked.
'The Volvo people,' Harpur said. 'In addition to the driver.'
'The front passenger – a suit, dark suit, collar and tie,' Madge replied.
'But you told us unkempt,' Harpur said.
'Yes, unkempt,' Madge said. 'A suit, neat, but still his features unkempt – like someone who'd been hanged. Who are *you*, anyway?'
'This is Mr Harpur, isn't it, seen on TV News after many crimes?' Al replied. 'They say like a fair-haired Rocky Marciano, that boxer years ago. I can see the resemblance now. Never lost a title fight.'
'Harpur's as straight as they come,' Iles said.
'Who?' Madge asked.
'Who what?' Iles replied.
'As straight as who come?' Madge said.
'In general,' Iles replied. 'All right, you don't let him near any woman you prize unless –'
'Any more about the driver?' Harpur said.
'For instance, Mr Harpur on TV after the shootings

146

down the Valencia,' Al said. 'People think you'll get bother at the trial, because of knowing in advance.'

'Obviously, when we could see him properly against the Mondeo, I got on the mobile,' Madge said.

'I thought a turf war,' Al said, 'but I didn't tell Madge to say this, because it would be speculative at that point in time. Just say about the body.'

'At first I didn't think it was the same man we saw in the main street,' Madge said. 'Someone torn and lifeless like that – it was such a difference from the smooth, frightening way he moved.' She stood again and seemed about to do another imitation of Vernon, but Al leaned over and pulled at an arm to restrain her. She sat down.

'That's dim, Madge,' Al said. 'If you're dead on your back you're not going to look smooth, are you?'

'Who else was present?' Harpur asked.

'A woman stood weeping,' Al replied. 'She'd suffered shock.'

'I think we've located her,' Garland said.

'When you see someone like that bleeding at a British kerbside shock is natural, even in this day and age,' Al said.

'Also a man,' Madge said. 'Forties. Al thought like Charlton Heston when younger. Me, he reminded of a lad who used to be on TV acting silly in a school cap – Cardew the Cad.'

'Profile,' Al said.

'I had an idea he knew the man in the gutter,' Madge said.

'Why?' Garland asked.

'Look, what I felt was – what I felt was he seemed really proud to be there,' Madge said.

'I didn't get that,' Al said. 'I don't know what you mean by that, Madge.'

'Proud?' Garland replied.

'Like he'd forced himself,' Madge said. 'Like he'd been scared but he'd fought back and now here he was, his voice too big and getting up really close to show he could, shoving his face almost against the other face – that is

I mean to show *himself* he could. You know what I mean? Like a kid making himself get nearer and nearer a barking dog.'

'Someone who'd beaten a panic?' Iles said.

'For the time being,' she replied. 'But all the time I thought he might go wobbly.'

'Nice clothes and shoes?' Iles asked.

'The man on the floor had great shoes,' Al replied.

'When I say he knew him, he pretended not to,' Madge went on. 'He talked about identification papers and behaved really surprised when I mentioned the walk.'

'Like sashaying?' Iles asked.

'You know both of them, do you?' Madge replied. 'Is this because you did, after all –'

'What happened to him?' Harpur asked. 'The one who got close.'

'Yes, very close,' she said. 'He wanted a real view of the wounds. That's what I mean – putting on the courage.'

'What happened to him?' Harpur asked.

'I don't think he wanted to be there when the cavalry arrived,' Madge said. 'Yes, quite good clothes. I don't know about the shoes.'

Al said: 'The shoes of the man on the ground looked to me as if –'

'A scar on his jaw,' Madge said. 'He fiddled with that, like he thought it might do a Vesuvius. Like a knife scar or falling on an open tin as a kid.'

When Madge and Al had gone Iles said: 'This is quite an experience for me.'

'In what way, sir?' Harpur asked.

'Being in an Incident Room with two men who were privy to my wife,' Iles replied.

'This would be at different times, sir,' Harpur said.

'Granted,' Iles said. He had that terrible calm and rationality about him which often preceded his worst convulsions. 'But tell me, Col – do you think there are many Incident Rooms in this country where that kind of meeting up has taken place, two shaggers around and an ACC cuckold?'

'To your credit, sir,' Harpur replied.

'What?' Iles said.

'Most ACCs never get to Incident Rooms,' Harpur said. 'They stay in the office with charts and budgets. I know how you detest jargon, sir, but I believe it can be said of you that you know "the sharp end", are very much "hands-on".'

'A certain restlessness,' Iles replied.

'Whose?' Harpur said.

'My wife's. Sarah's. At that time. Before we had our child.'

'I think so, sir,' Harpur said. He and the ACC found chairs.

'In that state, she'd take anything,' Iles replied. 'Often of an evening I'll spot a look of total mystification and sweet-natured amusement on her face now as she thinks back to the time with someone such as you, Col, with your garments.'

Garland said: 'My own view is that this gossip suggest-ing you orchestrated the killing, sir, is . . . well . . . gossip, and only that. I don't know about Mr Harpur, but I, personally, would not be surprised to find eventually you had very little to do with it at all, or even nothing.'

'Don't try creeping and smarming to me, Garland, you fucking destructive lech,' Iles replied.

A woman was shown into the caravan by the officer on duty outside and introduced as Gail Astey. She had a copy of the local evening paper's early edition with her. Harpur saw they'd got hold of a studio photograph of Sashaying from somewhere and it featured big on the front page. She was bright-eyed, a bit long-faced, but nice-looking in a gaunt, classy way. As far as Harpur knew, Iles did not mind class. The ACC twitched his legs. He took pride in their slimness. The woman was about twenty-four and had on a long sand-coloured woollen skirt and a shortie green jacket, also wool. Twenty-four would not seem too bad an age to Iles in some circumstances. 'I read about him and saw the car – the blood on the car,' she said. 'It's terrible. I noticed him in the Grenoble last night. I can't believe that rumour . . . well, would I be here if I believed the rumour saying you did it?'

'Who?' Iles asked

'The police,' she said.

'Thank you for your trust in us,' Iles replied.

'Someone called Iles,' she said. 'That name all the time.'

'Yes, I'm someone called Iles,' Iles said.

'I thought so,' she replied.

'Why?' Iles said.

'You seem the kind who'd feature big in rumours,' Gail said.

'Why?' Iles asked.

'I thought that as soon as I came in,' she said.

'Why?' Iles asked. 'Is it a matter of character, physique, skin?'

'As if you'd get many legends built around you,' she said.

'Thank you,' Iles replied. 'It can be a burden, though. Expectations.'

'I mean, why would you want to have someone like that slaughtered?' Gail said. 'The decoration on your shoulders – you're real brass, aren't you? My God, would people of that rank go in for such things? Incredible, surely. What are you? More than a sergeant, isn't it?'

'It's possible Garland here put this tale around,' Iles said. 'He hates me.'

She said: 'Hate? Why would –'

'I see you can't believe this, Gail, and wish to protest,' Iles replied. 'It's true, though. He's a dick on the loose and won't ever forgive me for breaking up his –'

Harpur said: 'How close to Vernon Templeton were you sitting last night in the restaurant, Gail?'

'Fairly.' She looked at the newspaper. 'What do they call him here?' She scanned the type. 'Yes, "Sashaying Vernon". They say he was known as that. Why?'

'Did you pick up any conversation?' Harpur asked.

'I didn't say he was with anyone,' she replied.

'Did you pick up any conversation?' Harpur said.

150

'You already knew he was there?' she said.

'What did they discuss?' Harpur replied.

'One name came up a lot,' she said.

'Oh, Christ, not mine, was it?' Iles said. 'This is what I mean about being legend material. Why are people so fixated on me? My mother always said I would be a centre of interest from many.'

'Denzil,' she replied.

'What about him?' Harpur asked.

'Do you know him – Denzil?' Gail said.

'What about him?' Harpur asked.

'I wasn't eavesdropping, you know,' she said.

'What about him?' Harpur asked.

'I didn't get much more. Just the name kept coming up. Denzil, Denzil, Denzil, but as if he was a problem.'

'How did the other man react when Sashaying mentioned Denzil?' Harpur asked.

'I didn't notice much about the companion, I'm afraid. He seemed a nobody. I mean against . . . against Sashaying – have I got to call him that? But he came back afterwards and gave me his card – a real bit of old time dirty-trickery – shake hands and pass the secret. Like spy stories. Ralph W. Ember.'

'Yes,' Iles said.

'Yes? Yes? How did you know?' she asked. 'So, it's true, you really set it all up? Hell, what kind of –'

'It's the tone of things that interests me,' Harpur said. 'Did they seem to be talking a policy, an agreement?'

'This newspaper says more or less straight out that Sashaying was a crook,' she replied.

'At a piffling level, but, yes, a crook,' Iles said.

'And the other?' she asked.

'Ralph?' Iles replied. 'Very much a pillar.'

'Of what?' she said.

'There was a structure in this domain,' Iles replied, 'a jolly regime of give and take.'

Gail stared at Iles. 'Look, have I been stupid coming here?' she said. 'You're running something. You don't need information, do you? There's not going to be any proper investigation, just some formal rigmarole.'

'Who's running something?' Iles replied.

'You,' she said.

'Having scrutinized the evidence, these two, Garland, Harpur, would hardly agree with that, would you, boys?' Iles said.

'I can tell you're distressed that the Mondeo and staining are still on view, Gail, but we can't move the vehicle until all our tests and so on have been made,' Harpur replied.

Iles said: 'My feeling is it would be best if I brought a car up close to the Incident Room and take you wherever you wish to go, Gail. In this kind of case, it's not always clever to be seen co-operating with the police. We could put my tunic over your head and face until we're clear. You might find it amusing to be swathed in an Assistant Chief's insignia.'

Garland said: 'Oh, I'll get one of our drivers to –'

'I don't mind taking Gail,' Iles said.

'Get into a car on my own with someone who concocts a death visit like that?' she said. 'Do I look fucking thick?'

'But you said you didn't believe we did it,' Iles replied.

'This was before I'd met you properly,' she said.

Understanding lit Iles's face for a second and then made it appallingly sad. Once or twice, Harpur had seen something similar happen before to the ACC. At these times more than during his rage spasms you could believe Iles capable of feelings, self-doubt, even humility. Harpur's daughters often claimed he had such qualities, especially Hazel, but Harpur thought it dangerous to accept any part of that and always tried to destroy their arguments. Now, Iles fingered the Assistant Chief emblem on his left shoulder as though disappointed he could not share it with this woman temporarily. 'Yes, it does unsettle people sometimes, having contact with me for a spell,' he said. 'My wife, obviously. But look, Gail, I'd ask you to be alert, all right? A caravan like this gets attention. You've walked down the street to it in daylight, haven't you? You're very observable. Somebody might want to know what you've been saying in here. They can't ask Harpur. He tells nobody anything, including me. They might set up circumstances to ask you, and they'd expect answers. A handshake with Ralph W. Ember in a public area – such communion might also be noted. Ralph is not necessarily safe these days, nor possibly those considered close to him. He realizes it and has lately made special provision for one of his children. If these two, Francis and Col, weren't the way they are I'd ask them to give you some protection, but I can't hand a lovely girl over to that kind of non-stop, invasive abuse. So, go alone, and go with vigilance.'

'You sound like a priest.' She stepped across the caravan suddenly and kissed Iles on the temple, an unhurried kiss. 'I thought I'd met you properly, but no. Now I have.' He smiled, reached up from his chair with one hand but did not actually touch her, as if he thought that would be forward. Iles looked shy, boyish, radiantly grateful.

'So, I *will* fetch a vehicle and you can get under my coat, shall I?' he said.

'Sorry, I don't think so. But thanks for your care.'

'Care is a big thing with the ACC,' Harpur said.

'Piss off, Harpur,' Iles replied.

In the night, Harpur went over alone to see Ralph Ember at the Monty. Ralph was usually there from about 11 p.m. until it closed around two. Harpur thought Ember took on a kind of dignity, even grandeur at the club. His smile then was a good smile, assured, not jittery. You could believe he had depth and a life plan. Hosting suited him. Roughhousing at the club, gun displays or blatant loot share-outs he never tolerated. Ralph demanded a civilized tone and achieved it now and then. Some would say oftener than that. People's idea of civilized varied. He ferociously disliked remarks pointing out the similarity of the name of the club and the title of a comic film about male strippers, *The Full Monty*.

Recently, on the advice of a staff member, he'd had a large, rectangular, inch-thick steel shield fixed to one of the

153

support columns in the Monty blocking any direct firing line from the club entrance to where he often sat at a small table behind the bar, checking accounts and suchlike, or merely imposing his presence. Ember had hired a local artist to do a kind of mural on each side of the metal, so that its role would not be frighteningly obvious. Facing the door, the shield showed a pleasant still-life with various richly coloured fruits, including oranges, limes and plums. On the reverse was a sunny beach scene, but no tit and bum, only a couple of blue and white fishing boats just off shore. Ralph prized taste. When Harpur entered the Monty now, he thought the still-life fruits looked especially high grade and mellow, perhaps because of new lighting. At the same time, the steel sheet did its bodyguard job, and he could not at once see Ember. Anyone wanting to blast him would have to come right inside and face the likelihood of identification and of possible lynching by members fond of Ralph regardless.

The club was crowded. The news of Sashaying's death like that, and near a dud car, must have disturbed some folk, making them seek comfort and security among friends. The Monty often provided this kind of healing function for members, though, as Harpur understood it, Ralph had resisted an after-funeral party for D.W. Sangster-Thame, despite his former membership. Ralph could be choosy. However, many saw the club as central in the city's social fabric. Harpur felt there must be folk in jail or on the run throughout the world who longed to be back among good-hearted comrades at Ralph's Monty. Now and then a big night at the club would suddenly develop when some member returned to celebrate release or acquittal. Ralph always kept a lot of champagne ready. Harpur knew there had been a party when Sashaying made bail. This was one of the troubles with bail – you were in the open and could get shot when on it, whereas a cell gave safety. Probably Sashaying's lawyers never thought of that. They were briefs and had a brief – to get him out. Lawyers did not always see the complete scene. Victories in court kept their fees up and made them QC, and this narrowed their view. Although Jill said she hated lawyers, Harpur thought she'd do well at the game.

'Ralph,' he said, 'the club's looking great. Mahogany, brass, all splendid, as ever.'

'Thank you, Mr Harpur. My strategy – if that's not too big a word – my scheme, then, is to bring in constant small improvements as and when I can, and hope these will meld with one another and give an overall upgrade.'

'And yet preserving the character.'

'I trust so.'

'Always a bonny atmosphere,' Harpur replied.

'Well, maintenance of that is what owning a club is all about, I feel. Harmony. Relaxation. Fellowship – to include ladies as well as the fellows, of course!' His voice was full and cheery.

'Mr Iles would have liked to visit with me, but being a fairly new father, he's keen to spend more time at home and share the duties if their baby doesn't get off to sleep – that kind of thing,' Harpur said.

'Ah, one remembers those times. Yet they were satisfying, as well as something of a constraint.'

'He asked me to give you his best.'

'Likewise,' Ember said. He had been in his customary spot but now stood and mixed Harpur gin and cider in a half-pint glass, two thirds cider, one third gin. Ralph poured himself a Kressmann armagnac and came out from behind the bar to sit with Harpur on a stool. 'Fatherhood probably brings a wholeness to Mr Iles's life that was missing previously. It's pleasant to watch something like that, I always feel, don't you, Mr Harpur?' He gave that steady, amiable smile, his jaw scar glistening.

'What was the Grenoble meeting with Sashaying about?' Harpur replied. 'And then more or less smooching the body in the street like that. You gone fucking mad, Ralph?'

'Has he forgiven all round, Harpur?' Ember said.

'Who?'

'Iles.'

'Did Vern want someone to run his firm when he was

inside?' Harpur asked. 'Or not simply *someone*, but specifically Ralph W. Ember.'

'For banging his wife, I mean. Has he pardoned you and her? It's not still happening, is it? She won't let you go? They can be like that. This is the thing about family life – it's sometimes only part of the picture.'

'I certainly don't think you did Sashaying or even set him up,' Harpur replied.

'Don't talk to me about people getting set up.'

Harpur said: 'Oh, some crazy rumours around, I know. If Mr Iles wanted to –'

'The Volvo was behind me all the way to the Grenoble.'

'Is that right?'

'I think they were after not just Sashaying.'

'Why would –'

'Look, you, personally, might not know anything about it,' Ember said. 'I'll admit that.'

'Thanks.'

'This could be way above your level. Staff College training. If Iles had something private going it would be . . . well, private. He's got people who would do anything for him. He might seem an out-and-out zany shit to the rest of us, but some stick with him. I see this as to do with the complexity of humankind, always fascinating.'

'What could he offer?' Harpur said.

'Who?'

'Sashaying. If he wanted you to uncle his operation while he's jailed, what's he putting your way? Just a percentage? Nothing more than that? Would you be interested? Christ, Ralphy, you're already doing around half a million. He's pennies.'

'This was a meeting without any concealment, Harpur,' Ember replied. 'Obviously I knew there'd be a blab to you, if you didn't know about it already, anyway.'

'Maria on your shopping list?'

'Who?'

'His girl. Were you warming to that for when he was gone? Well, now he's *really* gone.'

That grand smile came again. 'Do you know, Mr Harpur,

156

Vern's lawyers were truly impressed by the Monty,' he said.

'I should think so. Mahogany. Brass.'

'Their approval thrilled me.'

'Is that right?'

'These are people who've no doubt seen London clubland – are familiar with it. Or the man lawyer, anyway. Yet he noted the special excellences of the Monty.'

Harpur said: 'You're telling me you called the Grenoble dinner to ask Sashaying to –'

'This seemed to me an opportunity, Mr Harpur.'

'You thought Sashaying might –'

'I wanted him to sound out Matthew, his lawyer, to see if, given his high rating for the Monty, he could do some unofficial approaches in London, to get what's known as reciprocal facilities between us and clubs he might belong to up there. The Garrick has barristers, I'm sure. Or he might be in the Reform or Oxford and Cambridge. There's a lot of this goes on between clubs – reciprocity. If you belong to one of the Armed Forces clubs in London you can use the same sort of place in Australia or the States.' Ember gazed dreamily into his brandy glass for a moment. Then he spoke with solemnity. 'I don't know if I've ever mentioned my ambitions for the Monty, Mr Harpur. You see, I'd like to take it up to the category of what are known as "gentlemen's clubs" in the capital. A link established by Sashaying's lawyer would be a help, a move forward. As I explained, progress through gradualism. I think this a worthy aim, don't you?'

'The Monty's a fucking den of villains, wannabe villains and slags,' Harpur replied. 'Look at them. The lawyers would have smelled that. Nobody's going to tout this place in London, for God's sake. You must know it. This is not why you were at the Grenoble.'

'Banging the wife of an Assistant Chief for a protracted spell, Harpur – it can only mean he'll make sure you never get above Detective Chief Super, you sad, doomed sod.' Ember stood and went behind the bar again to mix another gin and cider and top up his own armagnac. A juke box

157

began to play some gentle ballads and a few people found space to dance.

'I was delighted to hear you'd been able to get Venetia back into Corton school, Ralph.'

'Thank you, Mr Harpur. It *is* a relief, for both her mother and me. Of course, they don't do the classics in the original languages despite protests but in these days of compromise and ruined standards I suppose I should –'

'Why should Iles want to knock over Sashaying and you?' Harpur said. 'Wouldn't he like to restore old ways? Ralph Ember was a main part of the old ways.'

'I hear he's coming up to his thirty years. He'll want to retire. He knows he's not going higher – same as you – despises himself for being an Assistant, won't hang about. Perhaps he's trying to get a monopoly state for himself and Manse Shale. Me and anyone else out of the way. He's always liked Manse.'

'An ACC, move into the trade? Oh, come on, Ralph.'

'But this ACC is ACC Iles.'

'Ralph, that's completely fucking nuts.'

'It would only be like how ex-government ministers get nice commercial jobs because they know so much about policy and methods from the inside. And don't forget the trade's on its way to recognition as all right.'

'Iles couldn't just move in there,' Harpur said. 'Shale works with a partner, doesn't he? He wouldn't let himself get ditched.'

'He's got an associate. Me, for now.'

'A partner. Isn't there someone called Denzil?' Harpur said.

'Denzil?'

'Does chauffeuring and bits and pieces, but that could be just cover.'

'Denzil? Don't know, but you might be right,' Ember replied. 'There *is* a chauffeur. He could be called Denzil. Not someone I'd get much contact with, so I wouldn't know. Where'd he get that name from – Denzil? But only a chauffeur, believe me.'

'You tell me you called the meeting with Vern, yet –'

'Yet, he paid,' Ember said. 'You've really had some whispers, haven't you? Or you've been nosing. Yes. He wanted to look big wheel. There was a girl in there at a table to our right and – this is going to sound vain, I'm afraid, Mr Harpur, but it's unavoidable – this lady's giving me the come-on all night although she's with a bloke. Embarrassing. It's that damn Charlton Heston thing. Of course, of course, Sashaying imagines it's all for him and has to act up. He can't flourish his dick so he whips out the Platinum Card card instead. I might reimburse his girlfriend before the account comes in. Did you say she's a Maria?'

Chapter Nine

Since the Agincourt Hotel meeting, Manse Shale had been depressed and stayed home a lot, but now the shooting of Sashaying Vernon really gave him back grand confidence in how things would work themselves out soon. Removal of Sashaying's face like that in an ordinary sort of street certainly sent a special message, but in Manse's view any kind of knock-over would of done. That rumour – the one claiming Iles arranged it all – it would be absolutely spot on. Behind such an attack had to be a true thinker. Often, even before this, Shale used to feel the Assistant Chief could be a professor of philosophy or political terrorism in a college. Manse decided he must get a meeting with Iles soon. This death was an obvious very personal invitation. It was like the killing said, *Here's what I, Des Iles, can do, Manse. Now, let's talk about* your *side of things.* To let him down would be harsh. In fact, it did not bear considering.

Probably, Iles would miss Sashaying's funeral, or Mansel thought he might of been able to get a word with him after the service or at the drinks and sandwiches. Police sometimes did attend funerals of murdered folk but this was when a best uniform show of sympathy and regret seemed due. They had been trying to get Sashaying sent down for menaces, though, so it would look ungenuine if senior officers joined the congregation in grief just because he was blasted ahead of that. Most probably it was Iles who had him killed, and this also might mean he'd stay away, though quite often after wastings of this vital sort the person or people responsible came to the funeral, part as

160

blind, part to sing 'Yea, though I walk in death's dark vale' and gloat.

It was true Iles as well as Harpur went to Curly Sambrook's funeral, and they must of known he was in the trade, though on the edge. But the service had been for Curly's child as well and Iles obviously decided a gesture was needed. Manse attended, of course, and he recalled it as a funeral where Iles behaved all right. Manse would definitely go to Sashay's funeral and do a reasonable wreath, somewhere around the £75 mark, but not in any special shape, such as a harp or Sash's favourite Airedale, like them naff East End gang funerals. Although Sashaying was only miniature in the trade, and although he had tried to set up something devious and shitty with Ralph via a dinner, he was part of the commercial landscape and deserved all-round support if eliminated.

Shale also loved that other bit of rumour saying Ralphy Ember should of got his, too, yet dodged out of it, as the sod always did manage to dodge out of disaster somehow. Foxy. This was a word Shale had come across for Ralph. Evidently he figured on a terrific list, though, and one day he'd be hit. All right, they said he'd stuck a pretty bit of armour plate up in his fucking riffraff club, the fucking Monty. But no armour could do a hundred per cent job. Ask King Harold – which definitely changed history. All right, Low Pastures, what he called his 'manor house', outside the city, was triple alarmed most likely, but alarms could not do a hundred per cent job, either. He loved to come the squire. Manse would give odds he contributed swedes from his 'kitchen garden' to the local church's Harvest Festival.

Obviously, Ember used to be more or less a mate as well as a trade associate, and Manse regarded him as all right in some ways. But why did the slippery dreg do dinner with Vern, then? Manse had commissioned a couple of subtle inquiries at the Grenoble and found Sashaying paid. So, a nice little wooing date, merger talk, you-and-me-together talk? And what was that scent of secrets between Ralph and Denzil Manse picked up not long ago and

161

which still tickled his nose? Ember was wondering about a new comrade, the treacherous prick, and had been auditioning?

Iles's scheme was plain to Manse and it delighted him, plumping up fast his morale again after them damn Agincourt let-downs. At that meeting, he was treated like some dud has-been, his flip-chart almost made a mockery of. Nearly all the esteem that night went to Ember for fixing the Valencia shoot with Harpur – if he did. Well, it didn't matter if he did or he didn't. The way things were, what was referred to as 'the perception' could be more important than the real thing. Perceptions were very well known these days. Ember had collected the Agincourt praise. Suddenly, Ralphy was the future and Manse nowhere. God, this hurt.

By great luck, though, one of Manse's most kind and understanding women named Patricia had been with him at the rectory then, and provided true comfort when she saw how bad he was damaged. Flip-charts Patricia absolutely appreciated though not a user herself in the kind of work she did. When Manse arrived home that evening from the Agincourt he had said straight out: 'Excluded, Trish.'

'I cannot believe this.'

'Excluded.'

'But why, Manse?' She was fully dressed. He hated returning home and finding any woman casual.

'Undercurrents,' he said.

'Which?'

'Alliances – not spoke about, but there.'

'Surely they know Mansel Shale is –'

'They don't want my methods,' he said. 'They will not admit the importance of major headings such as Enterprise, Co-operation, Order. They smirk. They think such topics are old wool, Trish.'

Shale believed totally in telling live-ins quite a genuine fraction of what took place on the commercial scene. This seemed only decent, proving a proper regard. If you invited a woman to share your home for what could be weeks or even months, they had some rights. These were not just bed and drinks in the garden on rural-style furniture, for heaven's sake. You talked to them. Manse despised men who kept their women out of trade affairs, unless, of course, the woman wished that. Some did. Manse did not go all the way with what was famed lately as 'the feminist movement' but he always kept in mind that women were unquestionably full human beings and should definitely be let into career matters up to a point. This was an aspect he and Ralph Ember very much agreed on. Of course, Ralph was long-term married, so he might tell his woman a bit more than Manse with such variables as Patricia, but the same idea.

'They're fools,' she had said.

'They believe they've found another way into the future through Ralphy Ember and Harpur.'

'Ralphy?'

'I was called into question,' he replied.

Although Patricia was not with Manse these days, another of his favourites had moved in, Lowri. That name showed she had a Welsh side, which Manse did not mind at all, even though his wife lived there now with some broker or newsagent or that kind of thing. In the old days, rectories were really big and Shale preferred it if he had someone to share the huge front bedroom and other areas of the property for a while since Sybil quit like that. Manse's house used to belong to St James's church and he liked to think of sermons or testimonials getting done in his den room, as he called it, where these days he would go over his accounts and then shred. The old Chief Constable, Mr Lane, had also lived in what used to be a rectory and Manse believed this helped them understand each other. It could be regarded as a kind of spiritual link. Lane had gone now, though. Shale considered it sad in a way that the Church was shrinking so much it must sell rectories. This explained why he enjoyed thinking of sermons hatched in his den. It gave like contact with better days for the Church.

Eventually, in the evening after Agincourt, Patricia had

said: 'Let's go and look at your Pre-Raphaelites, Manse. It will soothe, remind you that some values are eternal – the painters' values, yes, but Mansel Shale's also.'

Although grateful for her care he had remained down for a time. Now, though, he began to recover, and after the Sashaying news, said to Lowri: 'As I see it, Iles is clearing the way.'

'You seem excited, Manse.'

'Iles will retire. This is known.'

'"Clearing the way" for a new career?' Lowri asked.

'He won't stay on once he can hook his pension. He hates the new style with things. His power been chopped real bad. He won't wear that.'

'He's proud?'

'He got logic.'

'How do you mean, "logic"?'

'You heard of what's referred to as permissiveness, at all, Low?'

'Well, yes, like not too strict on matters,' she replied. 'The 1960s. Sex and the pill and so on, and saying "fuck" on TV.'

'Sex?'

'And other aspects of life.'

'Exactly. That's why I said logic,' Shale answered.

'In what way?'

'He's against it – permissiveness.'

'But I thought he and you and Ember –'

'He's against permissiveness like they're doing permissiveness now,' Shale said. 'This before was not *permissiveness*. This was an arrangement. Ember, myself, Mr Iles had an arrangement.'

'Right.'

'It was never spoke about, nothing like that,' Shale said. 'This was an arrangement that was like understood. You could not talk to someone like Mr Iles about something like that, he would turn all beefy and police. But it was like . . . well, yes, understood.'

'Between the lines.'

'What?'

'Understood,' she said.

'Exactly. You got it, Low. But now . . . now this permissiveness is different. Everyone can have a go because suddenly it's easier. This is not an arrangement, this is a scramble. This is not order and decent behaviour, this is grab and wipe out and get a bit of the turf – such as wild gunfighting down the Valencia, or Curly and his kid dead. All at once this lovely calm city is like Moss Side, Manchester, or Jerusalem.'

'Terrible.'

'We had a responsibility for this city in them days, Low. Me, I accepted that, no complaints.'

'This gave you a reputation.'

'So now you can see why I said logic, Low.'

'Logic?'

'Iles tells them, *All right, if you want permissiveness have your damn permissiveness. And when I get out I'll have some of that permissiveness too, why not if the law says it's nearly OK? I'm going to join up with a trusted pal, and we might create a monopoly.*'

After only a few seconds, Lowri saw it and clapped her hands twice in front of her sweet face: 'You, Manse. You're the trusted pal.'

He loved the way she said this – just like that, 'You, Manse,' not a question but the obvious. 'Mr Iles and me – we go right back, right, right back.'

'Great.'

'I don't think I'm shouting my mouth off if I say he trusts me. All right, he didn't like it I carried something at the Agincourt, but so were the others. You got to get equality or where are you, Low?' It did not matter how steamed up or sexual he was, Manse never got their names wrong. He regarded this as something worth taking trouble with, more than politeness – respect. You did not want a girl thinking she was only pussy and that it did not matter what name got stuck on it.

'Shout your mouth off, Manse?' Lowri replied. 'You'd never do that.'

'Some might think it strange for me to say about trust

165

when he's an ACC and I'm in the commodities, but it's always been good give and take.' At once Shale worried she might go wrong. 'I don't mean he ever been on the take, no way. But help to each other.'

'Look, are you really, really certain he sent that Volvo for Sashaying, Manse?' she replied. 'Is that what you're saying?'

'Not just me. A buzz. You ever heard the term "consensus", Lowri, meaning a buzz?'

'Yes, but you – do *you* believe it?'

'If you knew Iles, really knew him, you would see, Low, that a Volvo doing this sort of jaunt is absolutely Mr Desmond Iles, Queen's Police Medal. He's the kind who would keep the shooting until after Sashaying had a big feed, with wine, several veg, various cheeses, so he couldn't run too good, and if they only wounded him it would be more dicey in the operating theatre because he got a full belly. Iles is a refined brain. The name of his house comes from a poem, not some honeymoon spot, like Tarragona. He believes in peace and order just like always, so he wants all the others out of the way in plenty of time and while he still got nicely trained people he can ask to do it. This is four rounds in the face out of seven. That's very decent with a handgun in the dark, even from close. Sashaying gone, and Ralphy if it had worked better. This is going to be just Mansel and Mr Iles.'

'Has he said anything?'

'Who?'

'Iles.'

'He wouldn't,' Shale replied.

'You're guessing?'

'You ever heard of what's known as intuition, Low?'

'Like subliminal?'

'What?'

'Like sensing something,' she said.

'Sensing. Yes. Often, this is what leadership's about – picking up them signals others would miss.'

'That's a gift, Manse.'

'I think so. This is not something you can get from a

166

pamphlet or the Open University on television, which is fine in many ways.'

'But how do you make sure, really sure, like with the Volvo?' Lowri asked.

Probably Patricia would not of gone on like this, flinging the questions and doubts, but the thing about Lowri was she'd take it all ways with true pleasure, no faking, and never seemed to get sleepy. It could be a Welsh thing. People living in the hills with all the rain and the telly signal dim could most likely get fed up and have a go at all sorts. Sybil might be the same now, although she used to be so negative. Lowri was entitled to some time at the rectory. He stayed reasonable with her: 'This is the same as what I mentioned earlier, Low. This is something that if you put it into words it would disappear. This got to be just an understanding, for the present. Obviously, when he comes out and got his pension safe it would be different, most probably.'

'But when you go to meet him – well, how will you *show* him you can see what he's up to with blasting Vernon and maybe Ember if it had gone completely right?'

'This is why I say intuition,' Shale replied. '*He* got some. *I* got some. This will be what's referred to as communing. You've heard of communication, obviously, Low. This is like that, but without speaking any of it or writing any of it.'

'Like subliminal?'

'What?'

'Subconscious reaching subconscious,' she replied.

'Mr Iles is one who'd have a brilliant subconscious. The name of his house is Idylls which some pronounce to almost rhyme with his own name. But I don't think it's that at all – this is the communing I spoke about, communing with some poet from a different age, historical and yet alive for Mr Iles through his subconscious. That gun at the Agincourt – that could be another reason he wouldn't never say anything to me direct, for now. That gun might of worried him about me, but I can put this right in a conversation.'

167

'Conversation where, Manse? You can't go up to Idylls and ring the front door bell, can you?' Lowri said Idylls right, not like idols. This could be because she'd had plenty of schooling and knew the Idylls in a poetry book or because she heard Manse say it just now and remembered. Lowri chuckled about how crazy it would be for Shale to call on Iles at Rougemont Place, but she didn't mean to be cruel.

'What would he expect you to do, Manse?' Lowri asked.

'Who?'

'Iles. Does he want you to help what you called "clear the way"?'

'Just so he can know he got my approval and backing. This will be big for him.'

Shale would never mention to her, or even to Patricia if she'd been here instead, that it might be necessary to wipe out Denzil. Iles would not want Denzil around to fuck things up if Ember and Sashaying had been cancelled. This was why Manse saw a message in the Vern shooting. It was a message about Denz. It asked what Manse would do with him.

Because Denzil lived in a flat at the top of the rectory, he was like part of the family in a way, though with all his own facilities up there and what used to be the servants' stairs at the back of the house. Obviously, Manse did not want him coming in and out past the Pre-Raphaelite works all the time with remarks. Lowri would not be doing anything with him, Manse felt almost sure of that, because usually when Manse left the rectory Denz went with him, to drive. But she might feel shocked if she knew he'd been scheming and had to go. That was quite a thing when Iles found the Astra Modelo .38s on him at the Agincourt. He needed two? Probably, if Denzil was looking for an association in the new circs, Ember might be interested but he would also be worried about his daughter, Venetia. Christ, that name, though, Venetia – where did they find it, on a condensed milk tin? This was the girl Ralph brought back from France for safety. The tale went she liked older, seen-

168

it-all men. Denz would hear her calling him. Denz was safety?

'What about the other one?' Lowri said.

'Which?' Shale asked.

'The right-hand man.'

'Harpur?'

'He in on it all?'

'He lives down Arthur Street.'

'All right, but is he in on it?'

'That's what he's like – someone who lives in Arthur Street. He got no vision. No mind. He can write stuff in his notebook and read it out, but no thinking, not in a *real* way. His house just a number, no name at all. That's what I mean, Low. Now, you'll say Number 10 Downing Street is only a number, yet famous but there have been many film cameramen showing that number, so it becomes almost a name. Sometimes I feel sorry for Harpur.'

What Shale would never do as a way of meeting Iles like by accident was go down the docks and parts of the Valencia and try to spot him there. Iles did get to this area for a woman now and then, sometimes ethnic. This was known. But Manse thought it would not be in the spirit of things to bother him then. Decorum. Shale believed in this, and to dog Iles around those streets would be off colour. Some other way of meeting the Assistant Chief must be found. Besides, if he sort of bumped into Iles by accident at the Valencia it would look as though Shale also went there for pick-ups. He would hate anyone to believe that. He refused to take on girls in the open air, refused even just to talk with them about place or price. He considered any contact like that not on. Probably Iles would know Shale's feelings and find it unnatural to meet him loitering. Iles behaved toff. They said he came from some decent Protestant district in Belfast, not the Shankill. He never worried how people thought of him.

Manse knew he personally could not be the same. He was jumped-up and a flash-in-the-pan. He had to be careful, not just to make sure he was never seen poxed at a clinic waiting room, but he wanted no kerb-crawl court report in the Press either. Of course, Iles did not have to worry about getting pulled in by vice police, and he was the sort who'd think pox par for the course, so just get a dose of something to deal with a dose of something. Crabs he had definitely had. This was something else known, although he might have to meet the Queen at some official ceremony for a new dam or stadium and shake hands.

Denzil drove Manse to the funeral. Because it was this kind of occasion, Denzil agreed to wear the grey, chauffeur-style hat. Usually he'd kick up about that. Well, if you thought you was going to scheme your way into the prime job soon you would not want people to see you flunkeying. Shale took Lowri with him. He believed in that kind of thing. He thought that if a woman was into the cohabit spot for a while she deserved to get around with you to entertainments and events outside the home, also, when possible. Some of the other women, like Patricia or Carmel, might turn evil about this and jealous but, as Manse saw things, it was only the luck of this or that time, and if a funeral or wedding or christening came up while a particular woman was in residence at the rectory then that was the woman you went with. It could be any of them, no favouritism. Swings and roundabouts.

He found it a bit strange. There was no jealousy over him bringing another woman in for a spell and making love almost all over the property, as the others would obviously know – in the big bedroom, alongside the Pre-Raphaelites, on the major staircase, in the octagonal conservatory, across the sermon desk in the den. Only the trips to formal gatherings caused whining. Did women think the social aspect, like funerals or Charity Balls, meant more than sex?

They took the Jaguar, Manse and Lowri in the back. Shale left the partition open between Denzil and them as they drove. Lowri said: 'Manse thinks Iles, Denz.'

'That's the word,' he replied.

'What about you?' she asked.

Denzil's head twitched and he half turned for a moment to look at her. 'What?' he said.

'What do you think?' she replied.

'He could have some scheme,' Denzil said.

'What scheme?' she asked.

'There's Sashaying's woman,' Denzil said. 'I heard she got a lot of verve. Iles is into verve. He might want Sash gone.'

'Manse thinks a trade aspect,' she replied.

'Could be a trade aspect,' Denzil said.

'How?' she asked.

'Like that Deep Throat in the film said, "Follow the money",' Denzil replied.

'Manse thinks maybe Sashaying might have looked as if he'd mess up his prospects,' Lowri said.

'Whose prospects?' Denzil said.

'Iles's,' she replied.

'Iles wouldn't like that,' Denzil said.

'Obviously,' Lowri said. 'Or it could be someone else.'

'Someone else what?' Denzil asked.

'Who shot Sashaying,' Lowri said.

'Who says?'

'It's just something I wondered, for myself,' Lowri replied.

'Manse knows this trade. What Manse says is what really counts,' Denzil replied, 'especially when it's also what the buzz says.'

'If someone else thought Sashaying was getting into a business arrangement with someone that this someone else wanted to get into a business arrangement with himself,' Lowri said.

'A lot of someones,' Denzil said.

'Well, one of the someones would be Ralph Ember, wouldn't he?' Lowri replied.

'Would he?' Denzil said.

'Because he's the one Sashaying had dinner with,' Lowri said.

Shale stayed quiet. He would rather dodge all this. He was not sure he could speak to Denzil on such a matter

171

without showing that he had ideas about him and what he was up to.

'Are you accusing Mansel?' Denzil said.

'Manse? How?' she replied.

'Ralph and Manse have a business arrangement, haven't they? It's not a secret,' Denzil replied. 'Are you saying Manse came along and hit Sashaying because he was trying for a deal with Ralph?'

'Or someone else who wanted a deal with Ralph hit Sashaying,' Lowri said.

'Manse and Ralph, it's age old, isn't it, Manse?' Denzil replied.

'In a chaos situation there could be changes,' Lowri said.

'What do you mean, a chaos situation?' Denzil asked.

'So much suddenly on offer,' Lowri replied.

'What?' Denzil said.

'Trade. Prospects,' she said.

'Bringing us back to Iles,' Denzil said.

'Or someone else,' Lowri replied. Despite quite a collection of garments, she did not have funeral gear with her at Shale's house, so he had taken Lowri out yesterday and bought a good darkish trouser suit in fashionable needlecord – replacing denim these days. There was a cloche type hat to match, small, mauvish, with a darker ribbon around the base. Where Lowri was brought up women had to wear hats for funerals, if they were allowed to go to funerals at all, she said. This also could be Welsh, like the all-round love talents. Manse thought women's hats at funerals were OK, but there was no need for a rule. He always wanted women to express themselves – at funerals and altogether. Some women expressed themselves through hats, others by their hair, uncovered. But he did not mind coughing £89.99 for Lowri's hat. It made her look really pixieish and Manse enjoyed watching her leaning forward on the back seat of the Jaguar to tell Denzil, no messing, that she thought he or friends of his, not Iles, had done Sashaying. Manse himself still thought it was Iles but he believed in letting a woman come out with her own

172

notions, and, because of the expense and style, this hat didn't make Lowri's ideas seem any crazier.

In a way, it was best Iles should not show for the funeral, although Manse wanted to see him. Iles would be a great business colleague but Shale had to admit there were snags to him. Funerals brought these out. The trouble with Iles was sometimes he thought the service needed him and he would hijack the whole schedule – get into the pulpit regardless of the minister to give an address that was not always what folk wanted. The things he said might not be kind to the one in the coffin. He could of really upset Sashaying's girlfriend and family by giving unnecessary comments on his life, though true. Naturally, Iles was always going to be careful with comments about Sash's death, because Iles fixed it. But he would most probably of used remarks about the killing to push his own schemes for the future. Well, he was entitled to them schemes and the great thing was they might include Shale. However, many thought nothing else counted with Iles but Iles, Iles, Iles. It angered him if someone else collected more attention than he did, even someone dead. He was like an actor always trying to get himself more notice than all the others. Perhaps his mother focused on him too much as a child and now he missed it. You had to try to understand people's pasts as a guide to now.

'I hope you're not carrying those two Astra .38s, Denz,' Shale said. 'This is a funeral, you know, and in a sacred place.'

'How about you? You got your Heckler and Koch item, as favoured by police forces worldwide?' Denzil replied.

'I don't know whether Manse has or he hasn't,' Lowri replied, 'but for him it would be justifiable. Manse has . . . well, eminence . . . yes, eminence, and could be a target for all sorts.'

'Whereas?' Denzil replied.

Lowri said: 'There aren't many in his kind of position and I –'

'Whereas . . . whereas, I'm just the fucking chauffeur and

if someone wants to put bullets in me I don't have a right to answer back.'

'Who wants to put bullets in you?' she replied.

'You mean I'm not important enough?' Denzil said.

'You'd like to be *more* important,' Lowri said.

'I've got a nice number with Manse,' he replied.

'Yes, well appreciate it,' she said.

'You think I don't?'

'I think you should,' she replied.

'You saying I scheme?' Denzil said.

'I didn't hear myself say you scheme,' Lowri said.

'But maybe *I* heard you say I scheme,' Denzil replied. 'You'd say in front of Manse that I scheme?'

'Scheme how?' she said.

'That's what I'm asking you,' Denzil said.

'Just fucking drive, will you, Denz,' Shale said.

'I been smeared, Manse,' he replied.

'There hasn't been no smear, Shale said.

'She makes out I'm two-timing,' Denzil said. 'Ratting.'

'I can see you're hurt, Denz,' Shale said.

'I'd rather one of the others,' Denzil replied.

'Which others?' Lowri asked.

'Patricia. Or even Carmel. They wouldn't come out with questions and allegations,' Denzil said.

'It's not for some fucking chauffeur to compare Mansel's companions,' Lowri replied.

'Lowri was just talking general, wondering general, about who needs to carry a weapon,' Shale said. 'That was it, wasn't it, Low?'

'Did you say he had *two* .38s on him at the Agincourt?' she asked. 'That's supposed to be defensive only?'

'Here we are,' Shale said. 'Nice driving, Denz. You're one who can watch the road while conducting a pleasant chat with passengers.' This looked to Shale like it would be a very decent funeral. He could not see Iles here – that way he had of sitting in a pew all long-necked and staring, as if some of the worship around should be coming to him. There was a special hymn sheet with Sashaying's full name on the front and the years he covered: VERNON

174

CAPSTICK TEMPLETON: 1960–2003. Printed under the last hymn was an invitation: *The family hope you will join them for light refreshments after the service at the Matlock Suite, Capers' Inn.*

Shale wondered if Maria had tried for Ember's Monty. Now and then he allowed after-funeral parties. But Ralph did not like commodity people at his club, and especially not a lot of them at once. Shale had heard a word for this kind of attitude – 'compartmentalize'. Ember tried to compartmentalize. That is, he was a very major pusher but he was also the Monty owner, and he tried to keep them separate because one day he believed the Monty would turn into something fine and weighty and full of class. Fucking mad. Also, fucking sad to see him fool himself, whatever Manse thought of Ralph lately. Did Ralph really believe it? Of course, Maria might of decided she would like something chicer than Ralph's sweaty hutch in Shield Terrace, even if Ember was willing. The Matlock Suite would provide quiet elegance.

Manse definitely liked this church. What it had a lot of was character. Not every church you went into had character. He thought some churches were too churchy. He knew this would sound crazy if you said it to someone, but he could not stand churches and cathedrals that wanted to hit you with holiness, especially cathedrals. Some had sculptures of deads lying on top of tombs, stone hands together up under their chins, like praying for ever. And there might be little, separate chapels with their own altars and candles and all that, inside the church itself – it seemed over the top. This church for Sashaying was St Jude's, one of the saints not known to all, yet probably quite important or would he of got a church named after him in a good district like Meadow Gate? Lowri said he came just before the book of Revelation in the Bible. Although St Jude's had stained glass, faces in the paintings were not pop-eyed or pointy and they looked cheerful, no creepy religious misery. Shale could tell the timber for the pulpit came from a top-class tree. They had set it up high, so once the vicar stood there he could give out the hymn numbers or preach

175

and his voice would float along to everyone, even at the very back, and did not really need the mike.

'Friends, I want to tell you first that when I began to think about what I should say today, I met some difficulties. Of course, death is never an easy subject, but now and then it is possible to speak of a "good death" – when someone has gone after many years of useful life, or when the death has occurred during an act of bravery and self-sacrifice. I have to be frank and admit I cannot consider the death of Vernon Capstick Templeton at all like that. The full circumstances remain a mystery to me, and perhaps to all of us including the police. But what one must say is that it appears to be part of a regrettable, even terrible, pattern which has begun to harm our city of late. And it is with this in mind that I would speak my few remarks today.'

Shale saw Ember a few rows in front. He had all his family with him. This was smart. This was true Ralphy. This was to tell everyone that his contact with Sashaying had been absolutely legit, nothing to be ashamed of or to hide from his wife and daughters. All right, Sashaying had his rough side and might have been due some jail. But that wasn't nothing to do with Ralph – that's how Ralph would argue around it. That at the Grenoble? Just a business dinner, and tragic he got cornered in the little street straight afterwards, for reasons totally unknown to Ralph and no way to do with the meal.

And, in any case, Vern's trial had not come yet, so he could of still been innocent. It was not always easy to get someone for menaces because his friends or auntie could talk to witnesses and give them more menaces about what would happen if they went into the box and said there had been menaces. The thing about the truth was it depended where you looked at it from. This was the great thing with British law – the guilty was not guilty until the jury said they was guilty, and it did not matter how guilty the guilty was. This was one of the things that made Britain great when Britain was.

The vicar had got to what Manse knew must be the nub, and his voice went even stronger and swooped and dived

176

about under the high roof. 'Perhaps God is talking to us about the so-called permissiveness of our day,' he said. 'Yes, a modish word still, permissiveness. And in some ways a good word and a fine concept. But not a simple concept. We have to ask continually, don't we, where permissiveness ends and indulgence begins? Where, in fact, sin begins.'

Iles would of liked to hear permissiveness getting knocked, except, of course, the kind of live-and-let-live he used to run with Ralph and Shale in them grand former days. When you really got down to things, what most people wanted was order. The old Chief had wanted it. Now, Iles wanted it. And that was what the vicar wanted, too. But order took some fighting for and these days not everyone would fight for it – not this new Chief, for instance, and not some in the government itself, which was a fucking disgrace. In the congregation, Manse could see many street people from all the firms, most in clothes that seemed all right for a funeral. Sashaying was not big as a commercial figure but big enough to get a lot of loyalty through all the trade when dead. Delphine Haverson, across the aisle alongside Bart, had bent forward with her forehead on the back of the pew in front and seemed to be really giving things some weep. So, had Sash been helping her with the needs of the middle age situation at some time, before Maria or even during? Delphine would be a bit older but many men these days did not mind this too much, and with a name like hers she was almost bound to be older. It upset Shale to see her like that. She had on black leather mostly, as usual, and it looked wrong for someone in that kind of gear to cry so much. Manse thought of black leather as racy. Bart had his arm around her shoulders. It was strange for a son to be comforting his mother wearing leather in church because of giving it to someone like Sashaying. Manse hoped there would not be any harshnesses between her and Maria afterwards. Funerals could be like that. People would behave raw.

The patterer up in his hum-box was coming to an end, with some very good words about Vern as a person,

177

regardless. Shale felt glad. Maria and family members would get pissed off if all the preaching was only about Vern as a sign of bad times. To them Vern was just Vern. Someone must of told the vicar Vern's nickname and out came a kindly joke or two about that and the interesting way he walked, then a hymn and a last prayer before they took him away to the crem. It didn't matter then whether he used to sashay. In the porch, Denz said: 'Patricia's here, Manse.'

'Oh, fuck, where?' Shale replied.

'Is that important?' Lowri asked.

He had been a fool, worrying about Maria and Delphine, not his own women. 'What's she here for?'

'What's anyone at a funeral for?' she answered. 'To say farewell and show respect.'

'She doesn't know him,' Shale replied.

'But she'd guess Manse would be here,' Denzil said.

'What – she's spying?' Lowri asked.

'Patricia could be very fond of Manse,' Denzil replied.

'She wants to see who he's with?' Lowri said.

'Are you sure it was her?' Shale asked.

'Am I supposed to fucking hide or something?' Lowri said.

Manse had been thinking of going on to Capers' Inn, and had told Lowri and Denz they would, but now he wondered whether it might be best to cut that out, in case Patricia turned up there. This was the kind of thing Shale detested – women fighting about a funeral in a refined spot like the Matlock Suite. 'Perhaps she *did* know Sashaying, Manse,' Denzil said.

'In what respect?' Shale replied.

'Oh, are you jealous, Manse?' Lowri said.

'I mean, she had to have her freedom when not at the rectory,' Denzil said. 'That's how I understood it.'

'You understand fuck all,' Shale said.

'Not a child – Patricia,' Denzil said.

'You telling me she'd go to someone like Sashaying?' Shale replied.

'You *are* jealous,' Lowri said.

'Think of Delphine Haverson,' Denzil said.

'What?' Shale yelled. 'What?'

A man Shale had noticed moving among the crowd outside St Jude's seemed to hear the shout and turned to look. Manse did not recognize him, and that was a worry – why Shale had watched. At an outing like this, Manse wanted to identify everyone. This total fucking unknown suddenly approached now, tall, bulky, no nerviness. Oh, Christ, where was the Heckler and Koch? Did Denz have his Astra .38s? 'Are you Mr Mansel Shale? I was trying to find you. I'm glad you called out.'

Shale kept silent. He had not called out to *him*, the sly sod. He had called out from deep agony when Denz said Vern might have been seeing Patricia as well as Delphine Haverson.

'What is it?' Denzil asked this big clown. Denz did not produce anything, though. In one hand, anyway, he held that stupid chauffeur hat.

'I was given a description but it's difficult in such a large gathering.'

'A description why?' Denzil asked.

'My name is Peter Sangster-Thame,' he replied, 'father of Donald Wade Sangster-Thame, murdered in the Valencia district.'

'I heard about that,' Shale replied. 'Bad. Accept my sympathies. Excuse me if I was edgy. All sorts can get into a swarm like this.'

'Are you in the trade, too?' Denzil asked.

'I expect you can guess my purpose, Mr Shale,' Sangster-Thame replied.

'I wasn't there,' Manse replied. 'Stave Street. I can't remember the last time I was in Stave Street. Definitely not that night.'

'No, I am aware of that. I believe there was some kind of conspiracy, a deliberate orchestration of that incident, almost certainly involving the police. I wish to confront the authorities with this fact. Accordingly, I am trying to speak to all those prominent in the . . . in the business that my son unfortunately – tragically – chose. This occasion

179

seemed likely to draw many such. I seek any information they – you, Mr Shale – might have. I seek their – your – views. I particularly wish to collect a portfolio of such reactions before the trial of those who survived the Stave Street battle. Evidence of this kind might be à propos in some way, you see.'

'You're not another vicar, are you?' Denzil replied. 'No dog collar on, but the way of talking.'

Shale said: 'I got children of my own so I can understand a father wanting to find out about how his son was killed, but –'

Patricia pushed her way through a group on Manse's left. She was in an ordinary denim jacket and jeans, no hat. 'Tell me this, Mansel,' she said, 'did you ever take *me* to a funeral? I don't want you to rush. Think about it. Not just an answer off the top.'

'I don't believe a funeral ever come up at that stage,' Shale replied.

'Three times I've spent days, even weeks, at your place and you're telling me that there were no –'

'This isn't the kind of scene one wants outside a church,' Lowri said. 'In the circumstances.'

'Scene? What scene? I'm simply here to ask,' Patricia said. 'And you've bought her the gear, haven't you, Mansel, including a hat?'

Shale said: 'It's just that this death came along at a time when –'

'I'll talk to others while I may, if you don't mind,' Sangster-Thame said. 'Should you think of any information that might be helpful in my quest, perhaps you will telephone.' He passed Shale a card.

Glancing at it, Denzil said: 'Well, yes, a Reverend, but I'm not one to boast for spotting that. A boy like Donald must have been a grief to you – so small-time and then done this way.'

Patricia said: 'If you're the clergy, what do you think of it, bringing her here, yet while I was with him he –'

'Excuse me, now, would you?' Sangster-Thame replied and went to talk to Ralphy.

At the Matlock Suite, Manse became cheerful again. A very nice blue was how the walls had been decorated, darkish but still good, and a fine, thick blue carpet with thin silver and gold lines made a great match. He had decided they could come, after all. He thought Patricia would not show at a place like the Matlock Suite dressed like that, and when she had already done her talking outside St Jude's. He might phone her in a few days. He certainly would not send anything because he knew she'd feel he was trying to equal it out for Lowri's needlecord and cloche hat, and she would feel insulted to see it as a crude cheque. Also she was certain to wonder whether he would of bothered if Patricia had not found out for herself about the clothes. It was so vital to be sensitive when dealing with women. Some really deserved it. Patricia knew about prices and could probably tell the hat cost at least £89.99.

Although he would of liked to speak to Sash's Maria on his own, he knew this would be stupid from the jealousy angle after that difficulty with Patricia so he took Lowri over with him and introduced her. Denzil was at the bar. 'I thought the vicar doing the service was a right prick,' Lowri said, 'turning someone's death into a lecture on civic duty.' She had a sherry, Manse a beer.

'Thank you,' Maria replied. She didn't seem to be drinking.

'I didn't know Vernon, but I'm sure he was a considerable person,' Lowri said.

'You got it, Low,' Shale said.

'Thank you, both,' Maria replied.

Lowri said: 'People like the vicar believe that because they're –'

'Vern always thought well of you, Manse,' Maria said.

'Thanks,' Shale replied.

'But he'd heard you might be on the slide,' Maria said. 'We discussed this and discussed it.'

'Manse, on the slide!' Lowri said.

'You're bound to wonder what he was doing eating with Ralphy Ember,' Maria said.

181

'And Ralphy's not going to tell me,' Shale replied.

'Look, Manse, you come to the funeral and show your friendship even though you must have real uneasiness about what game Vernon was into. And I'm grateful for that, really grateful. You're such an eminence in our landscape, and it was wonderful to see you in the congregation – and Lowri, of course, of course.' Mansel felt true power in what Maria said and the way she said it. He could see why so many mentioned verve when they spoke of her. Verve had a lot of attractions. 'And that being so – my gratitude for your presence, Manse – I feel I must speak honestly to you. Anything less would be contemptible.'

'Honesty is a big quality in my book,' Shale replied.

'I want to state I've never believed the gossip that it was you sent the Volvo,' Maria said. 'Never.'

'Thanks,' Shale said.

'This would not be like Manse at all,' Lowri said.

'The Grenoble meeting was to do with the idea of you being on the slide,' Maria replied.

'Manse, on the slide!' Lowri said. She would do a nice show for him over and over, but Manse wondered if some of this idea got to her when she kept on hearing it. Lowri was like that – she could be awkward.

'Vernon picked up a whisper that Denzil might be thinking of a move against you, Manse.' Maria took half a step nearer to Shale and lowered her voice. There was a fair hubbub in the Suite to cover her words, but he could understand why she wanted precautions. Even when she came nearly down to a whisper Manse could still sense terrific verve in her. Obviously, he had to be careful not to show this or Lowri might turn rough again. 'Vernon didn't know how it might affect the scene if Denzil displaced you, Manse. And maybe Ralph felt uncertain, too. New alliances? Perhaps Denzil had spoken to Ralph but perhaps, too, Ralph was not happy with the idea of him as an associate.'

'It's possible,' Shale said.

'Vernon had the possible jail thing to worry about. He wanted someone he knew, so he goes to Ralph. I'm not clear about this next bit, Manse, because Vernon didn't really spell it out to me – he thought it best I didn't hear everything – you know, the way it is in the firms sometimes – protect someone by keeping her ignorant – but, anyway, I had the idea his deal with Ralph went like this – if Ember would look after things when Vernon was inside, he, that's Vernon, would arrange for Denzil to be done, so Ralph could take over that firm and have monopoly – perhaps with a share for Vernon when his time finished, and good living expenses for me and the children until then. They're with my mum today.'

It all come out in a real rush with plenty of breath and gulps, but Shale could follow it and knew she must be right. This was a girl not just with verve but a mind that could analyse. 'Thanks, Maria,' he said. To Shale, a statement like this had a true personal note. It was about the dirty scheming, yes, but also more than that. This was a woman speaking to a man. She became ashamed of Sashaying because of them plans, and, now he had gone, the only way she could get out from the guilt was to let Manse know the full evil she been living with so he could protect himself. This was a girl worth thinking about, especially if Patricia never came back through rage, and Lowri seemed dodgy and uncharming sometimes, also. Carmel, the last he heard, had one hell of a cough she could not get rid of and nobody with a rectory would want that around and knotted-up paper handkerchiefs.

Ralph Ember, his wife and the two daughters came over and Ralph and Margaret spoke some gentle comments to Maria about Sashaying. Maria was great and did not let on in her face or anywhere the kind of things she had just been saying to Manse and Lowri. Denzil joined them from the bar and there was some chatter and smirking between him and Venetia, though no actual body contact that Manse saw. You could never tell how far a couple had gone already. Maria went off to talk to other guests. Lowri and Margaret Ember began to chat nicely. Shale drew Ralph a little away.

'Delphine Haverson didn't come on, did she, Manse?

'Why?'

'Such a show. I hate that sort of behaviour. I told her not to attend the funeral.'

'What I never give credit to no matter what they say was that you was in on it, Ralph,' Manse replied.

'What?'

'Sashaying. The death.'

'Thanks, Manse. And ditto to you.'

'What I'm not is on the slide, Ralph.'

'Who would say you were?'

'I think of the Agincourt. People pooh-poohing large ideas and the flip-chart,' Shale replied.

'This was not something I noticed, Manse,' Ember said, the slippery slob.

'Denzil got no fucking chance whatsoever of taking me out,' Shale replied.

'Taking you out! Good God, some idea.'

'He does all right with your Venetia, I see.'

'Oh, a harmless little friendship,' Ember said.

'Yes?'

'A quite harmless little friendship, Manse.' Ember really watched them, trying to hear what Denzil said to her in case it was vulgar or an arrangement for later.

'I can get rid of him, Ralph,' Shale replied.

'Get rid?'

'That's it, get rid. The fucker deserves it. Well, you know the fucker deserves it. Didn't he come to you looking for partnering? I don't blame you, Ralph. Or not much. He's the one who would start an idea like that. You listened, I expect. You listened and never said a word to me. But all right, that could be just commercial practice. And then Sashaying. You listen to him, too. But I still don't blame you, Ralph. You swallow that wrong notion I was on the slide, so you get interested in proposals. Well, now the proposals are fucked. Sashaying's gone. Denzil's next. Sashaying was going to do Denzil for you after Denzil done me. Denzil's not going to do me although he got two Astras, I'll do Denzil. And then it will be only you and me again, Ralph. Now you can really understand I'm not on

184

the slide. I hate to see a heavy like Denz getting to make it with a lovely, young, bouncy kid like your Venetia.'

Lowri said: 'Margaret's mother can remember when there was an actual rector in the rectory, Manse, and jumble sales and a marquee on the lawns.'

'At all times when I'm using my den room or the drawing room I'm dwelling on the history of the house, Margaret, and, in my personal way, I try to honour it. I like to think I'm part of a tradition, you see. Not a church tradition, obviously, because I got a different career, but linked to a grand past through respect for the rectory building.'

'Often Manse will put a hand on the grey stone frontage as if drawing something from it,' Lowri said.

'Called communing,' Shale said.

The point about gents' toilets in a public building, even one like the Matlock Suite, was they could be very dicey. Manse remembered that fierce throat-cutting scene among the cubicles in the film *Witness* on TV. Generally, he would want Denzil to be somewhere close, but today Denzil could be part of the diciness. Manse went alone and was at a stall when he heard someone come in behind him. 'Mr Mansel Shale?' this voice said. He did not know it. He took his time before turning around, thoroughly zipped up again, no panic – leave panics to Ralph. Again a stranger, but surely to God it would not be another vicar, although some vicars did like this kind of spot and most probably called very matey greetings to likelies. He was smallish, wide, in a good dark suit, smiling like a peacemaker, very pale, thick-necked, big head. His accent seemed somewhere North – not Scotland but North, that rough sound, like to reach across fells. It did an echo in here, really snaking around cisterns. He said: 'I had a friend called Clement Liss Vayling, Mr Shale, killed in an area named the Valencia. Shot.'

'I've heard of him. This was a true tragedy.'

'Someone mentioned you knew a lot about goings-on in this town and might be able to help me find for a certainty who did it.'

185

'Who mentioned?' Shale replied.

'Probably there are others here who know a lot, too. That's why I put the Templeton funeral very much in my diary. When I say find who did it – obviously, we know who did the shooting on the night. But who laid it on, scripted it? This is what interests me and those who sent me. Don't say our fine, single parent friend Colin Harpur would be capable of that.'

'Capable?' It was not a place to stoke up chat with lead-on questions, but Shale had suddenly thought he saw possibilities. He kept things going.

'Yes, capable, Mr Shale. Two ways capable. Clever enough. Evil enough. Sambrook's woman thinks Harpur, they tell me – puts it around the hospital, bright with thanks. She's convinced. He's been up the ward, you know, and she's ecstatic about him. So, do I listen to her after all – see to him, maybe the kids as well, square the books?'

'No, you fucking don't,' Shale said. He had no firearm aboard, but Manse would never let himself get messed about by some big-voice outsider in a tiled Gents.

'All right, she's not the only one who says Harpur, and I –'

'Lay off Harpur, or I come looking for you,' Shale said. 'Lay off his kids, also. You got that? I'm good at finding people, especially people as shortarsed and ghost-faced as you.' Harpur was part of the old settled ways via Iles, the sweet bygone scene. Maybe Harpur would be part of *new* settled ways, if all that could be brought back. And it might be. Shale saw good signs. Everyone wanted order. But disaster for Harpur or his children would be a terrible slump towards more chaos, splintering all these grand hopes.

'I'm just telling you what I hear.' He held up both hands, like *kamerad*. 'Myself, I believe Harpur's pretty straight – that's what my research says, Mr Shale. Clever, but not devious clever, and for that Valencia project devious clever is what he'd have to be. Perhaps when the trial comes we'll

186

find out he could manage it. However, I doubt this, don't you?'

Although the suit was good, Manse could still see he had something under it. Manse did not mind. This lad showed the sense not to try anything like that with him. He looked a tidy sort of lad, even if he'd needed putting straight. This lad looked a handy sort of lad. Manse had a job for him, didn't he – an entirely non-Harpur job? Why not say after a decent hesitation or two that, of course, Clement Liss Vayling was done by one of the crew who'd been at Stave Street, but, yes, the planning came from someone else – someone present at the funeral, as a matter of fact, and famed for wildness, brutality and dirty ambition? Name, Denzil Lake, driver and dogsbody. It would not be true in the proper sense of true, or in any sense at all. Convenient, though. Did it matter who said goodbye to Denz as long as the goodbyes *were* said, and soon? Denz had it due and this boy in the fine suit would do to deliver it, no charge.

Stuff like that would need to come out slowly, bit by bit, like reluctant, or it would not seem believable to him, especially if he found out Denzil was Manse's chauffeur and general assistant. Get to the name, yes, of course, but not at once. Nothing like at once. 'You better be careful,' Shale said. 'This one carries two Astra Modelos .38.'

'Right. Who is he?'

'You might ask how I know for sure he carries two Astra Modelos. I seen them for myself at a companies meeting in the Agincourt Hotel.'

'Right.'

'One in each pocket of his jacket. He can deal with things whatever side they come from,' Shale said.

'Right.' He was getting jumpy. Well, understandable. Oh, yes. Someone could come in any time for a piss and find a murder chat.

But then suddenly Manse decided it would be yellow to give Denzil to some paid intruder – the kind of rotten thing Panicking Ralphy might try, a dodge out from true responsibilities. Manse wanted Denzil for himself. He was fucking *owed* Denzil for himself. If someone betrayed you personal, or tried to, you took him out personal. Basic. Basic. Shale saw maybe he'd already said too much. There were a lot of people at that Agincourt dinner, watching the Iles pile-up of guns. A busy researcher would probably get Denzil's name without any extra clues. He'd have to. 'Can't help you no more, sorry,' he said.

'But who? Where do I find him?'

'I told you, didn't I – can't help you no more. Why not bugger off home? Got a home, at all?'

Shale walked past him and out to the bar and Lowri. She deserved quite a bit of attention after that Patricia unpleasantness, and the soul-to-soul stuff from Maria most likely niggled her, also. Hell of a notable woman, Maria. Shale still felt cheery. That had been good – to ignore the holster bulge and say what he wanted to, and had to, regardless. This put right the moment of fright he'd had earlier when Sangster-Thame suddenly appeared. Christ, Mansel Shale scared by a vicar?

Chapter Ten

Iles said: 'In a way I admire him, Col.'

'Who?'

'The new Chief.'

'I know he thinks terribly highly of you, sir.'

'I mean, total fucking carnage on the streets and yet he sticks at it.'

'What?'

'Tolerance,' Iles replied.

'Perhaps he has to.'

'Why?'

'It's policy. Enlightened permissiveness is policy. The Home Office. The government,' Harpur said.

'Curly dead like that. The Valencia battle. Sash dead like that. Then Denzil Lake dead like that – his own pair of Astra pistols, both barrels in the mouth when found, but you still say no suicide?'

'Not unless he could fire the second one when dead from the first. Not unless there was no recoil to jolt the barrels out.'

'Symbolic, Col?'

'What?'

'Blowing his mouth apart,' Iles replied. 'Had he been talking to someone he shouldn't have been talking to?'

'Who? And who says he shouldn't?'

'Don't they notice these little incidents, Col?'

'Who?' Harpur asked.

'The Chief. The Home Office. The government.'

'I still don't accept you sent the Volvo, sir, deliberately to get more slaughter going and cause a policy retreat.'

'Thanks, Col. And now these trial people – Paderson, Liddiard, Dean – all acquitted and back in small arms circulation. I certainly don't blame you entirely for that. Certainly not entirely.'

'Thanks, sir.'

'And yet I think we're bound to triumph ultimately, Col.'

'Which we is that, sir?'

'You're with me on this, aren't you, Col?'

'On which?'

'Peaceful streets – a wholesome understanding with solid folk like Ralphy and Manse,' Iles said.

'That's gone.'

'But I hear those two are close again now. Full and fine reconciliation. My feeling is the civilized, practical accommodation will have to return. The deaths – someone's bound to see the reason for them eventually. Then there'll be an insistent call for us to come back, Col.'

'Which us is that, sir?'

'You're with me on this, aren't you, Col?'

'I see you as like General de Gaulle, sir – you know, waiting at Colombey les Deux Églises for the call to put things right.' They were in Harpur's living room, drinking tea. Iles had on a very tasselled new vermilion scarf with his tan bomber jacket, much richer for tassels than the old crimson one. Somehow, these extra tassels made him look more indomitable and clairvoyant than before with the sparser tassels. Harpur could definitely see why Iles kept his scarf on indoors here, except in really hot summers. The ACC was a scarf person and he recognized this, in his typically shrewd way, and went all out.

Denise, Hazel and Jill opened the door and came in briefly. Denise would drive the girls to judo and pick them up again later. Harpur liked all this domesticity. These last few evenings, his daughters had been more or less non-stop at judo, preparing for a competition. Denise was a true help ferrying them, almost a complete live-in, with responsibilities. Iles said: 'I love that gear, Haze. And Jill.'

190

'When we come back we're going to do something really special for supper,' Jill replied. 'Really, really special. Secret. Denise will show us. You can stay, Mr Iles. And with red *and* white wines.'

'They think you need bucking up, Col,' Denise said, 'after the trial disaster.'

'True,' Iles replied. 'Some performance.'

'But thank goodness no more killings,' Jill said. 'That Denzil Lake the last – so far. Dad, I heard Venetia Ember was *really* upset about him, I mean for absolute *days*. A friend at judo goes to her school and mentioned this. Venetia thinks her father did it – because Denzil Lake got too close to her, in her father's opinion, that is. You know what fathers can be like. Think of you and worries about Haze and Mr Iles.'

'Pus seepage,' Hazel replied.

'Ralph did him?' Iles said. 'Dear Ralph? Hardly.'

'We wondered. He's alibied,' Harpur said.

'Poor Manse Shale,' Iles said. 'What does he do without a chauffeur and general heavy?'

Denise said: 'Jill tells me her boyfriend's mother thinks things on the streets are now completely chaotic.'

'Yes, great, isn't it?' Iles replied. 'I've been saying the same to Harpur.'